"I meant to tell you that I really like what you've done in here."

Zaire wiped her mouth on the edge of her napkin. "I suppose you can tell that I love color."

He chuckled. "It tells me that you're not afraid to take chances."

She boldly met his gaze. "No, I'm not. Life is all about taking risks. We just have to be mindful of the ones we take. Regardless, we should learn lessons from the good and bad."

"I like that," he responded.

Tyrese was so close she could feel the heat from his body. His closeness was overwhelming.

Their eyes met and held. His eyes never strayed from her face, kissing her with his eyes. Zaire found the prolonged anticipation of the inevitable almost unbearable.

In one forward motion, she was in his arms. Tyrese kissed her hungrily.

The caress of his lips on her mouth set her body aflame. Zaire wound her arms inside his jacket and around his back. Her body tingled from the contact.

She gave herself freely to the passion of his kiss.

Abruptly, Tyrese pulled away, leaving her mouth burning with fire.

"I'm sorry," he uttered. "I never should have done that."

Books by Jacquelin Thomas

Harlequin Kimani Romance

The Pastor's Woman
Teach Me Tonight
Chocolate Goodies
You and I
Case of Desire
Five Star Attraction
Five Star Temptation
Legal Attraction
Five Star Romance
Five Star Seduction

JACQUELIN THOMAS

is a bestselling author. She has penned more than 45 titles
and writing is still her passion. She is currently at work
on the next installment of the Alexander family series.

FIVE STAR SEDUCTION

JACQUELIN THOMAS

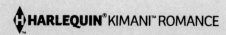

HARLEQUIN® KIMANI™ ROMANCE

Recycling programs
for this product may
not exist in your area.

ISBN-13: 978-0-373-86308-2

FIVE STAR SEDUCTION

Copyright © 2013 by Jacquelin Thomas

For questions and comments about the quality of this book please contact us at CustomerService@Harlequin.com.

Printed in U.S.A.

Dear Reader,

What do you do when you instinctively know that you have met Mr. Right, but he is not ready to admit that you're the only woman for him? Zaire Alexander is on a quest to find the answer to this very question in *Five Star Seduction*. Sparks ignite between Zaire and her new business partner, Tyrese Moore, from the moment they meet. Tyrese struggles to keep his feelings for Zaire under wraps, but soon discovers that love will always find a way of bringing two hearts together.

Five Star Seduction is the fourth book in the Alexanders of Beverly Hills series. I hope you have enjoyed getting acquainted with this wonderful family. It has been fun writing about their journey to love everlasting. What I've learned with each and every book in this series is this: when two people truly love one another, that love is worth fighting for. Wouldn't you agree?

Best regards,

Jacquelin

Chapter 1

The Alexander-DePaul Estate was considered the most coveted ocean-view home in Pacific Palisades. Zaire Alexander certainly agreed with the statement. She loved coming home to breathtaking, unobstructed ocean views from Catalina to Malibu in this commanding Mediterranean-style home.

Even now as she sat in the sunroom surrounded by her mother, sister and sisters-in-law, Zaire yearned to lounge by the pool admiring the picturesque surroundings.

"Livi, this is gorgeous," Zaire exclaimed, holding up a leather tote. "I really love it." She smiled at her sister-in-law. Livi and Blaze were still newlyweds, having only been married for three weeks.

"I know that red is your signature color," Livi responded. "So when I saw it, I thought it was perfect for you."

Zaire grinned and nodded. "*It's so me.* I can carry files, my iPad and laptop—just about everything I'll need for work."

She set the tote down on the sofa beside her and picked up another gift.

"That's from me, sis," Sage announced, rubbing the small mound of her stomach. "I don't think I included your card. I've been so forgetful lately."

"It must be the pregnancy," Zaire said, regarding her sister with amusement. "You have never been one to forget anything, especially if I borrowed your clothes or shoes."

They all laughed.

She opened the red-and-gold gift bag. "Wow, this is nice. A desk clock, a paperweight, mug…this is great. I can take this stuff off my list. Thanks, Sage."

"This last one is from Mama," Zaire announced as she ripped through the wrapping. "Ladies, thanks so much for this celebration. It's like a new career shower. Can you believe it? I'm actually starting my own company." She stole a peek out of the window to check on her brothers and her father, but they were nowhere to be found. Zaire returned her attention back to the women in her family.

Natasha chuckled. "We're so excited for you, Zaire. We just wanted to make sure that you do it in style, especially with your first big meeting with Tyrese Moore."

Her oldest brother, Ari, was Natasha's husband, and

they were also expecting a new baby in a few months. They already had a son, Joshua.

"Mama…" Zaire murmured as she held up a smaller box that was within the larger one. "Does this mean…?" Her voice died as she opened it. "Keys…car keys."

Screaming, Zaire jumped up and bolted toward the front door.

Her mother and the others followed, laughing.

A gleaming, vermilion-red BMW 640i coupe sat parked in the driveway of her parents' home with a huge black bow on it.

Zaire squealed with delight as tears filled her eyes. This was her dream car. She had not really expected her parents to buy it for her. "I can't believe it…. I just don't know what to say."

"I've never seen you at a loss for words, sis."

She glanced over at her oldest brother, Ari. "I didn't see you standing there."

He laughed. "I'm not surprised. I'm sure all you saw was red."

Zaire had been so focused on seeing her new car that she did not take notice that her father and brothers were all outside. They had been out on the patio playing basketball and enjoying a sunny August afternoon while the women gathered in the living room to celebrate Zaire's new business venture.

Filled with happiness, Zaire hugged her mother, and then ran over to her father and hugged him, too. "Thanks so much. I love you both."

Blaze walked down to where Zaire stood with their

parents. "I have this for you. I thought you might want to put this somewhere in your office."

"Blaze, you just lost your man card," Kellen, the youngest of the Alexander siblings, yelled out. "You need to stop with all of the sensitivity stuff. Only the women were getting gifts."

"Leave him alone," Sage told her brother. "I saw the present you gave Zaire last night when you thought no one was looking."

Amusement flickered in Kellen's eyes as he met Zaire's gaze. At twenty-six years old, she was a year older than Kellen. They'd shared an apartment in Atlanta while attending the same grad school. Although she was close to the rest of her family, she and Kellen shared a special relationship because they were so close in age.

Zaire eyed the beautifully framed photograph of their family and smiled. "Thanks, Blaze. This is definitely going on my desk."

"I have a gift for you, as well," Drayden announced. "I'm proud of you, sis."

She quietly noted that while she had inherited her mother's smooth chocolate complexion, she had her father's gray eyes, as did all of her siblings. Zaire and her family were very close, and they enjoyed friendly, smiling banter in a relaxed manner such as this.

For Zaire, this was what it meant to be a family.

Later that evening, after everyone had gone home, she sat in the family room with her parents and Kellen watching a movie on television.

"What time are you leaving in the morning?" she asked her brother.

"Around six," he responded.

"I bet you're glad to have the apartment all to yourself."

"Actually, I'm hardly ever there. Working on this thesis has been keeping me busy."

"I don't miss that at all."

Kellen shifted on the sofa. "I just keep reminding myself that I'm almost done with grad school."

"Stay focused," she advised.

"I am." He gave her a sidelong glance. "Now, what do you know about this Tyrese Moore?"

"Just that he started his own company five years ago as a boutique marketing firm, which has been very successful. I know that he's also involved in several different charities."

"Good luck on tomorrow," Kellen told her.

"Thanks."

Kellen pointed at their parents, who were both sound asleep.

Barbara lay with her head against Malcolm's chest.

Seeing them like that brought a smile to Zaire's lips. She was looking forward to the day when she met her soul mate.

Zaire chose a trendy black pantsuit to wear for her meeting with Tyrese Moore, the owner and CEO of the Moore Group. She strolled through the doors of 640 South, where the company was housed. The five-story building located on San Vincente Boulevard was considered Westside's premiere business location.

Her eyes traveled upward, admiring the dramatic two-story atrium. The select museum-quality art pieces throughout the building beckoned artists and art lovers from all over. It was apparent that Tyrese Moore was a man who appreciated art and the finer things in life.

"Miss Alexander…"

Zaire was jolted out of her reverie when she heard her name.

She glanced up into the most beautiful brown eyes she had ever seen. She broke into an open, friendly smile. "I'm sorry. I was just admiring the view."

She thought she detected a hint of a smile, but it disappeared before Zaire could be sure. She flushed when she realized that he may have assumed that she was talking about him. Although, he was extremely handsome.

"I'm Tyrese Moore," he said in a deep timbre. "I wanted to come down and greet you personally."

Her perfectly shaped eyebrows rose in surprise. "You're Mr. Moore?"

He chuckled. "You sound shocked."

Zaire gave him a quick and not-so-subtle once-over. Tyrese looked to be in his late twenties or early thirties. She hadn't expected him to be so young, but she did not give voice to the thought. "It's very nice to meet you, Mr. Moore."

Tyrese's smile was courteous as he guided her toward the elevators. "Pilar wanted to be here to welcome you herself, but she wasn't able to change her plans. She's still in New York."

Pilar Millbrook was Tyrese's partner and the person who had arranged this meeting with Tyrese.

They got off on the fifth floor.

"I'm very excited about this meeting with you," Zaire said. "Thanks for allowing me this opportunity to present my idea."

A smile remained on his extremely handsome face.

Why did he have to be so handsome? Zaire wondered. How was she supposed to focus with Tyrese Moore in her presence?

Tyrese's eyes landed briefly on the red leather tote as Zaire switched it from her right to her left shoulder. He noted from her overall look that Zaire was stylish, glamorous and she was definitely not afraid of color. Tyrese would bet money that she also drove a fancy sports car in red.

This was not the type of woman who played it safe, he decided. That quality made Zaire perfect for the direction in which he wanted to take the Moore Group. He could see why Pilar liked her. They shared similar qualities—they were both willing to take risks.

Tyrese knew that Zaire was the daughter of hotel magnate Malcolm Alexander, but this had nothing to do with his decision to meet with her. She was here based on her own capabilities.

He observed as she interacted with some of the other

employees. Zaire appeared to be unaware of the captivating picture she made when she smiled.

She glanced over in his direction.

Tyrese exchanged a smile with her, and then turned his attention to the young woman who suddenly appeared by his side. She carried a folder, which she presented to him.

He quickly provided his signature.

"Zaire, my assistant will show you to the conference room. I will be there shortly."

She responded with a smile.

His grin flashed briefly, dazzling against his dark chocolate complexion. "I'll see you in a few minutes."

As soon as Zaire entered the conference room, she sank down in a nearby chair to steady her trembling knees. "What am I doing here?" she whispered. She had been out of grad school for a few months and now she was about to present a bold proposal to a complete stranger.

Zaire hoped that Tyrese would keep an open mind. She had researched his company and had actually included it in her thesis—it was how she had met Pilar.

She already knew that Pilar supported her idea. Zaire just needed to convince Tyrese. If only his partner could have been in attendance. She could have used the extra support. Perhaps Pilar's presence could help distract her from the sexy man that she was meeting with. It was too late to run away now, Zaire decided. She would have to make the best of the situation.

Chapter 2

Zaire loved the large windows with a garden balcony in the conference room. They offered her a spectacular view of Beverly Hills, Hollywood Hills and downtown Los Angeles. She loved nature and the outdoors in general.

Shortly before ten, Tyrese appeared in the doorway. "I'm sorry about the delay."

"You're fine," she responded. "Your offices are very nice. I really love the art pieces you selected."

"Are you an art lover?" he asked.

When she nodded, he said, "After our meeting, I'll have my assistant give you a tour." His tone was warm and welcoming.

Zaire opened her tote and pulled out her pen, a legal pad and a proposal that she handed to Tyrese.

He took a seat at the head of the table.

Zaire stole a peek in his direction.

Tyrese once again captured Zaire's attention. His dark eyes framed his square face. His lips parted, showing a dazzling display of straight, white teeth. His profile was proud and full of strength, a quality that could be attributed to his commanding presence.

"As Pilar may have already told you, I am launching a high-end concierge service," Zaire announced. "Those who reside in the world of luxury are maintaining open-ended expense accounts for necessities such as client entertainment and personal lifestyle accoutrements," she stated. "What I have found is that a lot of these affluent families are looking for family excursions to help build schools in Africa instead of superfluous visits to privately owned boutiques and one-on-one attention at exclusive vacation resorts."

"And you are proposing a partnership with my company," Tyrese said as he reviewed the proposal in his hands. "Why do you believe we will be a good fit for one another?"

Zaire smiled. "The Moore Group was created to go beyond the typical marketing schemes. With over five years in the business of luxury marketing, you and Pilar have developed programs that allow you insider knowledge and access to what other companies may not be privy to—by partnering with me, you will be able to provide your clients access to things they may not have heard of or have access to."

"I hope this is not about lavish birthday parties," Tyrese stated.

"It's not," Zaire responded. "The message you will be sending by offering specialized or VIP client services is that the Moore Group recognizes what is going on in the world today, but we also have an understanding that certain clients still require high-end services."

"We are known for producing upscale events for our clients," Tyrese interjected. "Our mission is to assist our clients in building and managing their brand."

"Which can include tailoring experiences around their requests," Zaire said. "Whatever your clients desire, we can assist in making that idea a reality. VIP client services will be the epitome of luxury living, no matter how our clients define luxury."

"You've done your homework, I see."

"I wouldn't be here otherwise," Zaire responded with an easy smile. "You are a visionary, Mr. Moore. I would love to work with you in this venture. I'm sure there is so much I can learn from you."

"Please call me Tyrese. We are very informal around here. Tell me something. Why did you choose M.G.? We are not a big company."

"But you have done something most large companies are still striving to do—find a niche. You know your target audience and have concentrated on providing a unique but positive customer experience."

Tyrese pushed away from the conference table and rose to his feet. "Kaitlin will give you a tour of the rest of the building. I'll see you for lunch." He paused a moment before saying, "You did a great job. I'm impressed."

She warmed at the compliment. "Thanks."

Kaitlin was standing outside of the conference room when Zaire walked out with Tyrese.

"Ready?" she asked.

Zaire nodded.

He gave her a slight smile and walked in the direction of his office.

She resisted the urge to look back at him.

Zaire and Kaitlin took the elevator down to the first floor.

"Our screening room seats up to fifty," Kaitlin stated. "We also have a soundstage here on the first floor."

"I understand that there is also an exercise room and showers in the building, as well."

Kaitlin nodded. "They are located on the second floor."

They left the screening room and walked down the hall. "We have our own catering facilities here, as well. We often host special events."

"How long have you worked here, Kaitlin?"

"Five years," she responded proudly. "I was M.G.'s first employee."

Zaire smiled. "This company has grown very quickly."

Kaitlin agreed, "Tyrese has worked hard to make this a premiere marketing company for high-end companies like Mercedes-Benz, the Four Seasons and a host of others."

After the tour, Zaire was taken back to the fifth floor.

They found Tyrese in an empty room two doors down from his corner office.

"What do you think?" he asked when she walked inside.

Zaire glanced around the room. "It's empty," she responded.

"It won't be for long," Tyrese stated. "That is if you're willing to use it for your office."

She swallowed hard. "Are you saying that you accept my proposal?"

He nodded. "I'm having the contracts drawn up as we speak. We have all of this space, so I figured you might as well work here."

Zaire felt like hugging Tyrese, but she had to exercise restraint. "Thank you for this opportunity. You won't regret it."

"I look forward to a long relationship together."

She grinned. "Same here."

"You are free to decorate your office any way you like."

"Do you mind if I just hang out in here for a moment?" Zaire asked.

He smiled. "I have to leave for an off-site meeting. Stay as long as you like."

"Thank you again, Mr. Moore…Tyrese. I really appreciate your willingness to give me a chance."

"Pilar has a lot of faith in you. I have always trusted her instincts. I see no point in changing that now."

"I'll see you tomorrow."

Tyrese eyed her for a moment before breaking into a smile. "Tomorrow."

Zaire watched him walk away; his footsteps thundered down the hall. He was an extremely handsome man, but Zaire was determined to deliver everything she had promised. She vowed to prove herself a valuable asset to the Moore Group.

True to her word, Zaire was back in her new office bright and early. She noted that it had been thoroughly cleaned. A faint lemon scent still lingered in the air, and the hardwood floors gleamed.

Dressed in a pair of black jeans, a crisp white shirt and a pair of red sandals, Zaire took measurements of the windows, jotting down notes in between. She liked the platinum-colored side walls and had no plans to paint them another color. The back wall was painted a matte deep charcoal.

Zaire glanced down at her shoes and smiled. Red was the perfect accent color. She would use black-and-silver curtains in keeping with the theme, but her artwork and accessories would be red. She wanted a white desk to match the built-in bookshelves.

She turned around at the sound of a knock on the door.

"I didn't expect you to be here this early," Tyrese said.

"I'm an early riser, so I saw no point in waiting," Zaire responded. "I'm ready to get started."

"I'll have the contract for you to review by end of day."

She smiled. "Thanks!"

Zaire felt ripples of excitement at this new venture. She had originally planned to join her siblings in the family business, but then this opportunity had come around and Zaire just couldn't pass it up. It was the chance of a lifetime.

She had to admit that it wasn't just the business that excited her. Zaire was eager to get to know Tyrese. She was impressed with what she'd learned about him and totally entranced by his compelling personage.

She left the office to run some errands around noon. While she was out, Zaire decided to have lunch with Ari and Natasha.

Zaire pulled up to the Alexander-DePaul Hotel and Spa Resort in Beverly Hills. She handed the keys to the valet and entered through the revolving door.

Natasha was in the lobby when she arrived.

"Hey, you," Zaire greeted.

"How are things going?" Natasha inquired.

"Pretty good," Zaire answered. "I took a break from the unpacking. I can't wait to get settled. I'm so ready to get to work."

"Don't rush it," Natasha advised. "Enjoy the lag time for now."

They navigated to the hotel restaurant, where Ari sat waiting for their arrival. He greeted his wife with a kiss and then embraced Zaire.

It was obvious that Ari only had eyes for Natasha. He

had been married before to his childhood sweetheart. When April died, Zaire and the rest of the family worried that Ari would never recover from his grief. But then he'd met Natasha. She and her son, Joshua, had given him a reason to live again.

"Seeing you two making goo-goo eyes at one another like this makes me believe in love," Zaire said as she picked up her menu. "But if you don't quit, I'm going to start feeling like a third wheel."

Ari laughed. "That's because you are."

Natasha sent him a sharp glare. "Your brother is only teasing, Zaire."

"He's not, but I'm okay with it." She chuckled. "I'm hungry, and it's a good thing because he's picking up the tab."

When Zaire returned a couple of hours later, she found that her artwork had been placed on the walls and someone had unpacked a box of her books and placed them on her bookshelves.

Zaire glanced over her shoulder at the sound of footsteps. A young man dressed in a pair of navy slacks and white polo shirt said, "Hi, I'm Max. Tyrese asked that I help you with whatever you may need."

She noted that he didn't look much older than she. "Did you do this?" Zaire asked, gesturing toward the bookshelf.

He nodded. "Guilty."

She smiled warmly. "Thanks so much for your help."

"If you like, I can help you finish unpacking."

"Sure."

"So, what do you do here, Max?" Zaire inquired as they put away the rest of her books.

"I'm an administrative assistant."

"Do you enjoy your work?"

Max smiled and nodded. "This is the best company I've ever worked for. I was an event planner at my last job, but they had a lot of financial issues. A year later, the company closed."

Later that afternoon, Tyrese emailed the contract to Zaire, in addition to having his assistant hand deliver the hard copy.

Zaire went over the document, absorbing all of the information. She sat down in a chair she had borrowed from the conference room and opened her laptop.

She forwarded a copy of the contract to Natasha and her father's attorney. Zaire had already made up her mind to sign, but she wanted to have another set of eyes review the document, as well.

Zaire unpacked another box of books before leaving for the day. She walked to Tyrese's office to say good-bye, but he was not there.

She shrugged and then strolled down the hall to the elevator.

Tyrese was in the conference room. He saw her and gestured for her to join them.

Zaire stepped inside and quickly found a seat.

He introduced her to everyone and then moved forward with his presentation.

She noted that Tyrese seemed a different person when he was talking about his company.

"Someone asked earlier why we call ourselves a boutique marketing firm," he said. "We are a company that offers media outreach, media planning and marketing for all types of businesses. This includes corporations who have their own public relations teams. The Moore Group specializes in raising the overall awareness of a brand, product or image of a company or person. We determine a strategy that will best publicize the product that will drive traffic and boost sales…"

Zaire bit back a smile at how animated he was. His passion and love for his profession drove him tirelessly. She understood that feeling well. It was something they had in common.

She was impressed by his knowledge of marketing and public relations. Zaire was grateful for the chance to work with someone like him. There was much she could learn from him.

Her eyes strayed to his perfectly shaped lips.

Zaire flushed when he caught her staring and quickly averted her gaze. Embarrassed, she made a quick exit when the meeting ended.

Zaire was exhausted but pleased with how much she had been able to accomplish. If it had not been for Max, it might have taken her a couple of days. Her furniture would arrive tomorrow.

She drove along the Pacific Coast Highway with her

convertible top down. Zaire pushed back the strands of her hair dancing in the breeze.

She entered the house through the mudroom located off the kitchen.

"How did it go today?" Barbara asked when she walked into the kitchen.

"Mama, it was great." Zaire set her tote down in one of the counter-height chairs at the breakfast bar. "Tyrese Moore is a really nice guy, it seems. His employees all seem to love working for him. Pilar wasn't in town, but from everything she's told me I know that they are very close."

Zaire followed her mother out of the kitchen and into the family room.

"So what exactly will you be doing?" Barbara asked as she sank down on the sofa. She picked up the TV remote and turned down the volume.

Zaire sat down beside her mother. "I'm his partner. I'll be leading a specialized program that we are calling our VIP Client Services. It will vary from simply booking time on a chartered yacht or private jet to requests of creating a special evening on an island staffed with celebrity chefs and topped off by fireworks. Basically, no task will be too small or too large."

"So you partnered with his company in order to cater to the rich and famous?"

"Something like that," Zaire responded with a chuckle. "If this works out the way I believe it will, Tyrese, Pilar and I are going to all benefit greatly from our partnership."

Barbara smiled. "I'm happy for you, dear."

Zaire hugged her. "Mama, you don't know how much that means to me. I had every intention of working with Daddy until this opportunity came along—it was just too good to pass up."

"Honey, I understand and it's fine. Your father and I love you dearly. We taught all of you to think for yourselves and to make the best decisions for your lives."

"So Daddy isn't disappointed in me?" Zaire wanted to know.

"He isn't," Barbara assured her.

Later, in her room, Zaire searched through her closet to find something to wear the next day. She decided on a pair of gray slacks with a bright yellow silk shirt.

She washed, blow-dried and flat-ironed her naturally curly hair. Zaire intended to wear it in a sleek style, so she wrapped it. She hardly ever wore it straight, but she was in the mood to try something different. This change in her was motivated by Tyrese Moore.

Zaire had developed a crush on her new partner. Tyrese intrigued her.

When they had had lunch together yesterday, Zaire had noticed that every now and then Tyrese displayed what she could only consider a secret expression. He was kind, professional and passionate about his work, but extremely private when it came to his personal life. He had been dubbed by the press as elusive, which contrasted with his choice in profession.

A couple of times, she'd felt the heat of his gaze on

her, but Tyrese had been careful to avoid being caught looking at her for any long period.

He was attracted to her. Zaire was sure of it, but she was also pretty positive that Tyrese would never act on that attraction.

She felt a certain sadness at the thought.

Tyrese remained in his office long after everyone else had gone home, which was not unusual for him. He was normally the last one to leave and the first one to arrive.

The telephone rang.

He picked it up without taking his attention from his computer monitor. "Hello."

Silence.

"Hello," he repeated.

Tyrese waited a moment for a response. When there was none forthcoming, he was about to hang up.

"Ty…it's me."

His mouth took on an unpleasant twist. "What do you want?"

"I want you to give me a chance to explain."

"I don't want to hear anything you have to say," he snapped. "I'm tired of this. I told you to never call me," he said, his mouth thinning with displeasure. "You need to respect my wishes."

"Please," the woman pleaded on the other end of the line. "Please don't hang up on me. Ty, I know that you loved me and I want you to know that I never lied about loving you. I meant every word. I—"

He cut her off by interjecting, "No, I'm not doing this with you. Do me a favor and never call me ever again."

"It's been five years, Ty. There is something you really need to know. You don't know what I had to go through to find you."

"You needn't have bothered," he replied. "I thought I was clear. I never want to see you again." His face felt tight with strain. "Just leave me alone."

"It's not that simple, Ty."

"You ruined my life with your lies and manipulations. What's done is done. I would say that's pretty cut-and-dried."

Tyrese hung up.

Although he hated to admit it, even to himself, the call had unnerved Tyrese. He wanted no reminders from the past. Instead, Tyrese wanted to focus on the present and the future.

His mind centered on Zaire. She represented the future of his company.

Tyrese took a deep breath and exhaled, adjusting his mood.

He admired Zaire and her enthusiasm. She had entered the spotlight after publishing her thesis highlighting the unique approaches M.G. took with brand marketing. One of Zaire's professors had attended college with Pilar and had sent her a copy of the paper.

Tyrese was surprised initially that Zaire had decided not to follow in her father's footsteps. It was fortuitous for his company that she had come to him with her proposal.

Even now, he could feel the warmth of one of her infectious smiles. He was extremely attracted to Zaire. Tyrese cautioned himself to be careful around her. The last thing he wanted was to have to face a sexual harassment charge.

Chapter 3

"How are you enjoying your new career?" Sage asked as she and Zaire sat down to eat lunch a couple days later.

"I love it," Zaire said. "There's a lot to learn, but everyone has been so great. This is such a great opportunity to partner with someone like Tyrese Moore straight out of grad school."

"I'm kind of surprised at that," Sage said. "Not that you're not qualified. We are now a part of that world that you're catering to, so you do have firsthand knowledge."

"I think that's why I'm perfect for it, although we weren't raised with silver spoons in our mouths. But I think it takes a person familiar with privileged lifestyles to lead a program like this."

Sage nodded in agreement. She took a sip of her

water before asking, "So, what do you think of Tyrese Moore? Ryan says that he's nice but keeps to himself mostly."

Zaire broke into a grin. "He's so handsome, Sage. I have to remind myself all the time that he's my partner. He's been in New York for the past couple of days for meetings with prospective clients. I have to tell you— I'm glad he's gone. I need some time to gather myself."

"Yes, you do," she murmured. "Especially since you work with this man. But at least he's not your boss. That would definitely be frowned upon."

Zaire's expression stilled and grew serious. "You and Ryan fell in love when you thought he was just some guy you'd found on the streets. That was a workplace romance. Look at Livi and Blaze. Same thing."

"Our relationships were different, Zaire," Sage said. "You and Tyrese will have to work closely together."

"I don't see a problem with that," Zaire commented.

"Zaire, I'm just saying that you have to be careful. That's all. Tyrese has his other employees to consider, as well. The last thing you want is to be the subject of workplace gossip."

"I don't care what other people think," she uttered. "But I get what you are saying."

"Keep your relationship out of the office," Sage advised.

"I hear you."

Zaire finished up her meal.

As they walked out of the restaurant, Sage said, "I hope I didn't upset you."

"You didn't," Zaire assured her. "You gave me something to think about."

"I'll support you no matter what you decide." Sage checked her watch. "I need to get going, sis. I have a prenatal appointment, and Ryan's meeting me at the doctor's office."

Zaire placed a hand to her sister's round belly. "Take care of my little niece or nephew."

They embraced.

"I'll see you this weekend," Sage said.

"Family cookout," Zaire responded with a smile.

"I really want you to be happy, sis."

"I know that."

After Sage got into her car and drove away, Zaire also left.

Her sister was right. She was going to have to keep her developing feelings for Tyrese under control. Zaire did not want to be the subject of workplace rumors.

Tyrese was glad to be heading back to Los Angeles. He always enjoyed his visits to the Big Apple, but he preferred the less frenzied pace of the West Coast population.

"We will be taking off in five minutes," the flight attendant announced.

"Thank you," he responded, and then returned his attention to the documents in his hand.

The company plane, a Boeing 767, looked ordinary on the outside, but Tyrese had had its interior outfitted with chestnut and decorated in a rich burgundy and gold. The small conference table on board bore the company logo in the middle. The plane had been redesigned to carry twenty-four passengers.

Tyrese stretched and yawned in his seat. He settled back against the soft leather and closed his eyes.

Images of Zaire floated behind the lids. Tyrese had called to check on her, but they'd only had time for a quick conversation because she'd had to get to a meeting.

His mouth curved into an unconscious smile.

He felt movement as the plane glided down the runway.

Tyrese was looking forward to seeing Zaire. He gave himself a quick reminder that he could not allow himself to get involved with her. She was his partner. She could never be more than that to him.

The last time he'd gotten involved with someone within the company, it had cost him his job and almost his business reputation. Tyrese's mouth took on an unpleasant twist.

That experience had provided the motivation for going into business for himself. When no one would hire him, Tyrese had relocated to Los Angeles and started his company, which had proven to be very successful in what he termed boutique marketing. He was labeled a visionary, a man of the future.

The old adage was right as far as he was concerned. Success *was* the best revenge.

Zaire walked out of the Zumba class wearing a smile. She patted her damp face with the back of her hand.

"You're the only person I know who leaves a work-out with a smile on your face," Livi said, shaking her head in disbelief. She dabbed at her neck and chest with her terry-cloth towel.

"I always feel good after a workout," she responded. "Don't you?"

"I'm exhausted and sore."

Zaire glanced over at Livi. "Let's stretch some more. It'll help."

Livi smiled blandly. "Sure."

They headed over to a corner that was vacant.

"We have a gym at M.G.," Zaire said. "I've been thinking about exercising there at least two days a week when I'm working late."

Livi gave her a puzzled look. "M.G.?"

Zaire reached out, stretching her muscles. "Yes, that's what everyone calls the company."

She straightened to relieve the ache in her shoulders.

"What are your plans for this evening?" Livi asked as they headed to their cars a few minutes later. "Blaze and I are having dinner at the Chart House. You're more than welcome to join us."

"Thanks, but I think I'll just head home. Daddy's in San Francisco, so I'll order some takeout for me and Mama. We can make it a girls' night."

"Okay, I'll talk to you later. Please give your mother a hug for me."

"I will," Zaire promised.

In the car, she placed a quick call to her mother.

"How do you feel about Italian for dinner? I can pick up some on the way home."

"That sounds great," Barbara said.

"Great. I'll be there shortly."

The red lights on a plane in the air caught Zaire's attention as she waited for a light to change from red to green.

Tyrese is flying back to Los Angeles tonight.

The thought thrilled her.

His absence from the office had been duly noted by Zaire. Tyrese was very hands-on, but he was careful to avoid micromanaging his team. He was well respected by everyone in the company and had a reputation of being fair.

Zaire wanted a peek into Tyrese's life outside of work. There was no mention of a woman in his life, although she knew he most likely kept his personal life completely separated from the company. He aroused her curiosity. Zaire vowed to find out everything about Tyrese Moore.

Tyrese was already in his office working when Zaire arrived the next morning.

She knocked softly on his open door. "Good morning."

"Come in," he said. "I want to hear how everything went yesterday with your meeting. Bill Daniels can be temperamental, but I heard that you had no problems winning him over."

She sat down in one of the visitor chairs. "He was

actually a very nice man. The meeting went very well. I have some ideas that I think will work great for his venue."

He smiled. "Great. I can't wait to hear them."

Zaire rose fluidly from her chair. "I guess I'd better get to work. I should have a proposal ready in a few hours."

Tyrese checked his watch. "Why don't we meet around three to go over what you have?"

"Sure. I'll see you then."

He leaned back in his chair and appeared to be studying her.

Their eyes met and held.

Tyrese broke the unspoken connection between them. "Zaire, I don't want you to feel pressured. If you find that you need more time to put together your proposal, just let me know."

"I don't foresee a problem," she responded. "I'm meeting with Bill and his partners on Friday to give the presentation, so I would like to test it on you since this is my first real client." Zaire headed to the door. She paused briefly to say, "I'll be ready for our meeting today."

As soon as she walked into her office, Zaire summoned her assistant. She had requested that Tyrese allow Max to work for her. He'd conceded without an argument.

"I need you to get me a list of the top ranches in the country. Bill Daniels loves horses and the outdoors. I think if we can find a ranch with corporate facilities, it would be the perfect venue for a retreat."

Max nodded. "There are some great facilities in Denver."

She opened her laptop and prepared to get started on her project.

Zaire scanned the notes from her meeting with the owner of several car dealerships. Bill Daniels wanted to depart from the annual retreat in Miami. He wanted something different that would require more than just sitting around a pool drinking champagne. He had become more health conscious after he'd suffered a minor stroke. Bill wanted his management team to experience a weekend of healthy foods and activities designed to keep them physically fit.

She made a note to put together a list of the top personal trainers in the country.

Zaire settled back in her chair, deep in thought.

She really wanted this first project to impress Tyrese. Zaire also wanted to prove that she was indeed the right person to head the program. She knew that some of the employees believed she had been chosen because of her family connection to Robert DePaul. Regardless, Zaire intended to prove herself.

Max burst into the office. "I think we have the perfect venue for the retreat."

"Where?" Zaire asked.

"The eight-thousand-acre Willow Creek Ranch in Granby, Colorado, has two hundred horses for riding the terrain, tennis courts and golf."

"Sounds good, but does it offer anything in the way of spa treatments?"

Max nodded. "Aching muscles and bruised egos can rejuvenate themselves by way of massage therapy and a Jacuzzi tub. There are even indoor and outdoor exercise areas."

Zaire pulled up the website on her laptop. "This is very nice, Max. Great job."

Max arranged to have lunch delivered to the office so that he and Zaire could continue working on the proposal for her meeting with Tyrese.

She was determined to capture his full attention with what she had come up with.

Chapter 4

"As you can see, the Willow Creek Ranch is perfect for what Bill Daniels has in mind for his company's retreat," Zaire said. "There is a lake for fishing and walking trails."

Tyrese gave her a smile that sent her pulse racing.

"I have to say that I think you nailed it. I like the idea of having a personal trainer and a nutritionist on board."

"I can also arrange to have the chef prepare health-conscious meals all weekend if Bill wants. He really wants this retreat to be fun but also educational. He wants his managers to start thinking more about their physical well-being. He is hoping that they will also encourage their employees to do the same."

"It's actually a great idea," Tyrese said. "We have

an increasing problem with obesity, which is leading to serious health issues."

Zaire agreed, "I think more and more companies are focusing on the health and well-being of their employees. We may get more requests like this in the future."

The telephone rang.

"I need to take this, but don't leave," Tyrese told her.

She studied him while he talked to Pilar. Rumor had it that she was planning to relocate to New York and open another division of M.G.

The mystery in his eyes beckoned to her irresistibly. There was an air of efficiency about Tyrese that fascinated her.

He ended his call. "I'm sorry about that."

"It's not a problem." Zaire stared with longing at him.

Every time his gaze met hers, she could feel her heart turn over in response.

Zaire noticed that Tyrese was watching her intently. She cleared her throat softly. "I've taken up enough of your time. I should get back to my office."

"You have nothing to worry about when you have your meeting with Bill."

"Thank you."

Zaire's gaze landed briefly on his lips. She wondered what it would feel like to kiss him. Her pulse quickened at the speculation, prompting her to pick up her pace as she headed down to her office.

She was entirely too caught up in her own emotions. Zaire deliberately tried to shut out any awareness of him as she finished the rest of her workday.

* * *

Tyrese had to fight his own battle of personal restraint where Zaire was concerned.

It was an awakening experience that left him with a feeling he had thought long since dead.

He had to regain control of his emotions before they led him back down a path of ruin. Tyrese had worked too hard to make M.G. the company it was. He was not about to let his attraction to Zaire destroy his life's work.

Tyrese checked his watch. He needed to leave now if he wanted to be on time for his dinner with Pilar.

He made a couple of phone calls before leaving the office.

Pilar was already at the restaurant by the time Tyrese arrived.

"So tell me, Tyrese," Pilar said as they sat down at a corner table. "What do you think of Zaire Alexander?"

"She's everything you said she was," he responded with a smile. "She has drive, and she's ambitious."

"Zaire is also very beautiful."

Tyrese looked at his longtime friend. "You and I go way back, Pilar. You know everything about me, even what happened in Chicago. You also know that I can't go back down that road."

"I'm not saying that you should hook up with Zaire," Pilar stated. "But you do need a life outside of M.G."

"I'm fine with the way things are," he said softly. "It's probably better that I stay single."

"What happened in Chicago was not your fault,

Tyrese. She lied to you. You can't stop living your life because of your past."

"I don't want to talk about it." His tone was firm and exact.

"Okay." Pilar's smile did not indicate compliance. She continued, "So, let's talk about our plans for expanding M.G. I believe that New York is the perfect location for our East Coast division."

"Marshall doesn't want to relocate?" he asked.

"No, he doesn't." She sighed. "Tyrese, he's asked me to marry him."

"I hope you said yes."

Smiling, Pilar held out her hand to show him the four-carat princess-cut diamond solitaire on her left hand. "We're getting married in six months. We both want a big wedding, and we're having it at the boathouse in Central Park."

"I'm really happy for you, Pilar."

"So what do you think about a New York division of M.G.?" she inquired.

Tyrese broke into a grin. "Let's do it. M.G. is just as much yours as it is mine. You worked as hard as I did to make this a reality."

"Are you serious?"

"Yes. You'll run the East Coast division, and I'll oversee operations out here."

"I can't put into words how much this means to me, Tyrese. I love you dearly."

He smiled. "I love you, too. It's because of you that

I never missed out on having a sister. You have always been there for me."

"I feel the same way about you. I will never forget the day you went after those boys who stole my bicycle. They nearly beat you to a pulp, but you didn't give up. You brought my bike back to me."

Tyrese laughed at the memory. "It didn't belong to them. I was not going to let them keep it. It took two days for me to steal it back."

"You are such a wonderful person, Tyrese," Pilar murmured. "I just wish you'd open your heart. Let someone love you."

He shook his head. "Let's not go there."

"Tyrese—"

"No, Pilar," he said. "Don't worry about me. You focus on yourself. As for me, there is no room for romance in my busy schedule."

They finished lunch and headed to the office.

The very moment that Pilar and Zaire saw one another, they embraced and settled down in her office to catch up.

Tyrese had a feeling that he wouldn't see Pilar for a few hours.

Smiling, he made his way to his office. He would catch up with Pilar later that evening. They were having dinner together at his house.

"We feel confident that the Willow Creek Ranch can provide one of the most successful experiences ever for your group...." Zaire said as she paced back and forth across the floor of her office.

She turned around to find Tyrese standing in her doorway. Strangely, it came as no surprise to see him there.

"I was practicing my presentation."

"You have nothing to worry about," Tyrese said. "You're a natural."

Zaire rewarded him with a smile. "How long have you been standing there? Did you hear my whole presentation?"

"Pretty much," he admitted.

She folded her arms across her chest. "So what do you think? Honestly."

"You did a good job," Tyrese said.

"But I want it to be great," Zaire responded in earnest. "What can I do to really make this shine?"

He pointed to her laptop. "Don't use visual aids as a crutch. Strategically place visual aids in your presentation to highlight the major points. Trust me—your style and personality will have much more impact."

"Anything else?" she asked.

"Don't let him conclude the meeting with the idea of getting back to you, Zaire. We want him to determine the next steps right then before life gets in the way." He smiled at her. "You are going to do a fantastic job."

"Thanks. Will you or Pilar be here for the meeting?"

Tyrese nodded. "We both plan to attend, if you don't mind."

"I welcome it," Zaire told him with a smile. "I'd like to see your friendly faces in the room."

He was so handsome in his navy suit that her breath practically caught in her throat. Zaire swallowed tightly as she averted her gaze. She needed to maintain her focus and mentally prepare for her meeting with Bill Daniels.

Chapter 5

Zaire paced back and forth in her office again. The meeting with Bill Daniels and his team was in an hour. She had gone over her presentation all the previous evening and then again that morning.

"You're going to wear a hole in the rug," Max said. He walked into the office, carrying a mug of something hot. "I brought you some herbal tea. I thought it might soothe your nerves."

"Thank you, Max."

"I have everything set up in the conference room. As you requested, I ordered lunch and it will arrive promptly at noon."

"Great," Zaire murmured. "I can't wait for this to be over."

"You're going to do fine," Max assured her.

She sat down at her desk. "I'm so nervous."

"You shouldn't be. You are going to nail this—you've worked out a perfect weekend retreat."

Max's predictions were correct.

Bill Daniels enthusiastically clapped his hands at the end of Zaire's presentation, which prompted his partners to do the same. "I have to say that it takes a lot to impress me, but you have managed to do so. You've planned the retreat with an emphasis on a healthy lifestyle for our company."

"Then we should get it on the calendar," Zaire stated. "I don't want you to miss out on your preferred dates. I can book the ranch this afternoon."

"Sounds good," Bill said.

Max arrived with lunch for everyone.

"In keeping with your goals for health and wellness, I've ordered a light lunch of grilled chicken and spinach paninis, vegetarian BLT wraps and a delicious antioxidant salad for lunch." Zaire stole a peek at Tyrese, who gave a slight nod of approval.

After lunch, Pilar came to Zaire's office.

"Bravo," she said. "Tyrese and I thought the presentation was outstanding."

"Thank you."

"Zaire, I wanted you to know that I will be relocating to New York, but I am only a phone call away if you ever need to talk to me. We are making the announcement soon. We're opening another office."

"Congratulations, Pilar. This is wonderful for you, although I had hoped you would become my mentor."

"I can still be your mentor," she assured Zaire. "I have to meet with Tyrese shortly, but I wanted to stop by and congratulate you. Let's plan to have lunch one day next week."

The telephone rang minutes after Pilar left the office.

Zaire answered it.

"How did it go?"

"Kellen, it went great. Better than I ever expected, actually."

"I'm proud of you, sis."

She broke into a grin. "Thanks. So what are you up to?"

"Just got home from the library. I have a date later on."

"When do you not have a date?"

He laughed. "Hey, don't hate."

"Whatever…"

"Well, I know you're still at the office, so I won't keep you on the phone. I'll give you a call one day next week. I may need your help with my thesis."

"Okay. Just let me know."

Zaire hung up, grabbed her purse and left for the day. She felt like celebrating.

Saturday morning, Zaire was up early, helping her mother prepare for the cookout.

"I need to find a place of my own," she announced as she retrieved a covered pan laden with raw fish from the refrigerator and set it on the counter.

Barbara glanced up from her cooking. "You don't have to be in such a rush to find an apartment, dear."

Zaire sat down on one of the barstools at the breakfast bar and opened up the classified section of the newspaper. "I know, Mama, but I really want my own place. There are some really cute apartments not too far from the office. I really need to do this for me."

Barbara nodded. "I understand. You're ready to leave the family nest."

"I am," Zaire confirmed. "Kellen and I have lived together for three years and now I'm back home with you and Daddy. I'm ready to find a place that's totally mine."

"Do you mind if I help you look?"

"I would love it, Mama."

Two hours later, Zaire opened the door for Ari and his family. All of the family except for Kellen would be joining them for a weekend of fun and food.

Eyeing her sister-in-law's swollen belly, she asked, "Natasha, how are you feeling?"

"I get tired a lot, but I'm fine."

Sage and Ryan arrived a few minutes later.

"I thought Blaze and Livi would be here by now," Ari stated as he opened the subzero fridge. "They were leaving around the same time we left." He grabbed a bottled water and opened it.

"They'll be here shortly," Barbara announced. "I asked Blaze to stop by the store to pick up some barbecue sauce and more eggs."

Zaire moved about the kitchen, helping her mother

apply the finishing touches to the meat. Ari carried it outside to the grill.

Livi entered the kitchen, carrying a shopping bag.

Barbara relieved her of the burden. "Thank you, dear."

Zaire left the women in the kitchen to join her nephew on the basketball court. "What's up, Joshua?"

"Nothing."

"What's wrong?" she asked, noting the unhappy look on his face.

"I want to play football, but Mommy said I couldn't. Dad said that I might get hurt." He stole a peek over his shoulder before adding, "I think they're scared that I might get sick again."

Zaire blinked back tears. Eight-year-old Joshua was in remission from leukemia. Just two years ago, he was not able to attend school because his blood counts were low, putting him at risk for infection. Joshua was able to keep up with his friends and class work via satellite. The chemotherapy treatments placed him at risk for long-term effects that included bone thinning, severe joint pain and possible joint replacement. His doctors had informed Ari and Natasha that he would have to be monitored for at least ten years.

"Honey, we love you so much, and we just don't want anything to happen to you."

"All of my friends play football. I want to do it, too."

Zaire glanced over at Ari.

He came over to where they were standing. "Son, I've been talking with your mom, and we've changed our minds. We are going to let you play football. I want you to know something else. Uncle Drayden is going to be one of the coaches."

Joshua's face lit up.

"I need you to understand that you are not going to play all four quarters yet. You have to listen and do what you're told. Remember what the doctor said about the effect of the chemo on your bones."

"I'm gonna be real careful, Dad." Joshua looked up at him. "Thank you for trusting me. I'm not gonna do something to end up back in the hospital. Besides, I believe that God has cured me of leukemia. We don't have to be scared. I'm gonna go talk to Uncle Drayden about football practice."

"You've made your son really happy," Zaire told her brother.

"Wait until he finds out that he is only playing a few minutes each quarter, if that. Right now, it's only going to be until halftime."

"I don't think it'll matter. Joshua just wants to be a normal little boy."

They settled down to eat.

Zaire sat down beside Sage.

Ari cleared his throat loudly. "Before we get started, I have an announcement. I was going to wait until after we ate, but this can't wait." He looked at his wife and broke into a wide grin. "Natasha and I just found out that we are having twins."

"Congratulations," Zaire yelled out.

"Do you know the sex?" Livi asked.

Natasha nodded. "We're having a girl and a boy."

Joshua was delighted. "I wanted a brother and a sister. Now we don't have to have any more babies. I'm glad 'cause Mommy isn't any fun."

Zaire bit back her laughter.

"I don't know what we're going to do with that little boy," Sage whispered.

"We're going to have to watch him play football," Zaire responded.

Sage glanced over at her. "So, they changed their minds about letting him play?"

Zaire nodded. "Drayden is coaching his team, and Joshua's only going to play for a few minutes per quarter. Starting off, he's only going to play until halftime."

"I think it's a good idea."

She agreed, "I know they are afraid he'll get hurt."

Sage smiled. "Natasha is going to have him so padded up, he'll probably bounce if he falls to the ground."

Zaire laughed and then took a bite of her hamburger.

She decided to take a stroll on the beach after lunch. "I'll be back shortly," she announced. "I need to walk off some of this food."

Sandals in hand, she walked slowly, relishing the feel of the wet sand beneath her bare feet.

"Zaire..."

Her steps slowed, and she turned around. "Tyrese, I'm surprised to see you. Do you live around here?"

He shook his head. "I was at a party nearby. It was

getting wild, so I thought I'd take a walk before I headed home. I love the ocean."

"So do I," Zaire said.

"Would you mind if I walked with you?" he asked.

She couldn't help but notice the tingle of excitement inside her. "No, I don't mind at all."

Tyrese glanced over his shoulder. "Do you live in the area?"

"Right up there," she said, pointing to the top of the hill. "At least for now, anyway. I'm actually looking to move closer to work. I'm not crazy about the morning traffic."

He nodded in understanding.

"Are you always so quiet?" Zaire blurted.

He chuckled. "I never really considered myself quiet."

"Surely you don't believe that being talkative is one of your qualities? I realize that you're a very private person, but you're also extremely quiet." She could hardly tear her gaze from his profile.

"I suppose it's part of my nature."

"Tyrese, I apologize if I'm being intrusive," Zaire stated. "I've only ever worked with my family, and we talk about everything."

His mouth curved with tenderness. "You're fine."

Mixed feelings surged through her as they walked.

"I met your grandfather once," Tyrese said. "At a charity event. I had just started my company, and Robert DePaul was very encouraging."

"I hear that a lot," she said. "I wish I could have met

him. I hate that we didn't find out that he was my father's biological father until after his death."

Zaire did not want to bring up work, but she had run out of things to say. She did not want to start tossing questions at Tyrese about his personal life, although she yearned to learn more about him.

"You've gone quiet on me."

Zaire glanced up at him. "I am trying not to overstep my bounds. However, I must confess that I'm dying to ask you questions about you—especially since we're partners."

Tyrese laughed then. "What would you like to know?"

"What do you do for recreation?" she asked. "Do you like sports?"

"I like basketball."

Zaire stopped walking. "Can you play?"

"Not as much as I used to," Tyrese answered. "Work keeps me busy."

"You need a life," she blurted without thinking.

"Excuse me?"

"Outside of work, I mean."

"You are something else, Miss Alexander."

"I just believe in a well-rounded lifestyle. It makes you into a better person." Zaire found herself extremely conscious of his virile appeal. She tried to assess his unreadable features.

She caught sight of someone running toward them. "That's my brother."

They waited for him to catch up.

"We were getting worried," Drayden said between tiny gulps of air. "I figured I'd come looking for you."

"I'm sorry," Zaire said. "I ran into my boss on the beach. This is Tyrese Moore."

Drayden smiled and offered his hand. "It's nice to meet you."

"I guess I let time slip away from me," Zaire reasoned aloud.

"I'll see you in the office on Monday," Tyrese said. "Enjoy the rest of your weekend."

Zaire smiled and nodded. "You, too."

"You do know he is your partner?" Drayden reminded her as they made their way back to the house. "You don't play where you work."

"What are you talking about?"

"I think you know."

"Drayden, you've gotten the wrong impression. I just ran into Tyrese on the beach. What should I have done? Not walk with him?"

"Sis, I just don't want you to get hurt."

"I won't," she responded thickly. "I'm just getting to know my partner—there's nothing wrong with that."

"Just be careful."

"Are you okay?" Sage inquired when Zaire sat down beside her on the patio. "You look upset."

"I'm fine," Zaire huffed. "Drayden just needs to mind his business."

"What happened between you two?"

"It's nothing I want to dwell on." Zaire settled back in the lounge chair, disappointed.

* * *

It was a challenge for Tyrese to keep Zaire out of his thoughts. Running into her on the beach had not helped the situation. This was the first time he had seen her with her hair in its curly state. The soft, dark curls were windblown, adding to her exotic appearance. The denim shorts showed off her perfectly shaped legs.

Zaire was outgoing and vivacious. Tyrese liked those qualities about her. He was sure that she rarely met strangers because she was so friendly. He had never been that way. If it had not been for Pilar, Tyrese probably would not have had many friends. They were always together growing up, so her friends simply accepted him. Zaire possessed a freedom that he had never fully experienced.

Tyrese silently hashed out a number of reasons why he could not risk getting involved with Zaire.

His cell phone rang, cutting into his thoughts.

He glanced down at the screen, noting that the caller ID was blocked.

"Hello…"

"I'm glad you answered your phone."

"How did you get this number?" he asked. Tyrese had just changed his number a few days ago. It was supposed to be private.

The tide rolled up closer to shore, wetting the bottom of his pants. Tyrese resumed his pace. "What do you want?"

"I have resources, Ty. Honey, I just want to talk to

you," the caller said. "There's so much I need to tell you."

"What we had is long over," he stated. "I don't know why you can't get it through your head. I want nothing to do with you. The truth is that I should have followed my gut instinct in the first place."

"You still love me, Ty. I know it."

"You're delusional if you think I still have feelings for you. I've moved on, and I've started a new life for myself. Take my advice and do the same. Goodbye."

Tyrese ended the call, and then he decided to walk back to his parked car.

He glanced upward when he neared the house Zaire lived in. He could see a group of people standing near the brick enclosure.

Tyrese had not met Malcolm or Ari Alexander, although he had heard a great deal about them. He had considered approaching them in hopes of gaining their business, but before he could, Pilar had already connected with Zaire.

He'd liked Zaire instantly. She appeared honest to a fault, which he found to be a rare trait. His past relationships had been filled with lies, deception and manipulation. They had left a bad taste in his mouth. The last real relationship had taken him a couple of years to recover from, both personally and professionally.

It was for this reason that Tyrese would never get involved with Zaire. She was now his business partner, and he vowed to never cross the line with her.

He glanced up once more at the Alexander home

overlooking the beach and Pacific Ocean. He released a long sigh in resignation.

There was no point thinking about a woman he could never have.

Chapter 6

Zaire glanced up from her computer monitor just as Max walked into the office. "There is a Harold DePaul here to see you."

She stared at her assistant in astonishment. "Really?"

Max nodded.

"Bring him in," Zaire stated. "I can't wait to find out what this is about."

Her family's history with Harold had not been a positive one; however, Meredith had informed them that her brother wanted a chance to redeem himself. Zaire and her family were willing to give Harold that opportunity, although they weren't quite sure of his sincerity.

"Nice office," Harold murmured when he strolled in a few minutes later. "I like the red accents."

"Thanks," she responded. "What can I do for you, Harold?"

"I'd like for you to coordinate a weekend retreat for my management team. We usually go away to one of the properties in Hawaii, but I'd like to do something different this time."

"When would you like to have the retreat?" Zaire asked, picking up a legal pad and a pen.

"Normally, we go in September. This will be for the retreat next year."

She gestured for him to take a seat. "What have you done in the past?"

Zaire made notes while Harold talked.

"We spend most of our time in workshops. This time I really want the retreat to focus more on engagement."

"Any preferences for location?"

"The island atmosphere works well, so somewhere exotic and tropical," Harold stated. "My managers have worked hard, and I'd like to reward them for their efforts. We will still have some workshops, but I want the focus to be on recreation and relaxation."

Zaire nodded in understanding.

After their meeting, she walked Harold to the lobby.

"I appreciate what you're doing."

He shrugged in nonchalance. "I have no doubt you are going to make this retreat the best my company has ever seen. Billy Daniels has been bragging non-stop about you."

Harold's words made her smile. "I'm glad he's pleased."

He paused at the entrance. "I look forward to working with you, Zaire."

She smiled. "Same here, Harold. Oh, it would be really nice to see you at one of the Alexander cookouts. Your sister comes when she and her fiancé aren't away on some romantic getaway."

Harold broke into a wide grin. "I'll check my calendar."

Zaire headed back to her office. She found Tyrese waiting outside her door.

"You've been here a little over a week and you've already picked up a new client," Tyrese said with a smile. "I like that."

"Thank you."

He followed her inside.

"I take it things are better between Harold and your family."

Zaire met his gaze. "You know all about that?"

Tyrese nodded.

"He's changed a lot. Harold's no longer contesting the will. There was really never any point in the first place." She waved her hand in dismissal. "I'm just glad it's all over with."

"Shouldn't you be leaving for the day?" Tyrese inquired, looking at the wall clock.

Zaire shook her head. "I'm going to work for a couple of hours more. I'm in meetings most of tomorrow, so I'm trying to get as much done today as possible."

His eyes swept over her face. "I'd better head back to my office. There are some things I need to take care of."

Tyrese's cell phone started to ring.

She watched him with a critical squint. He glanced down, and his expression changed right before her eyes. Zaire could tell that the call had angered him.

He rushed out of her office without a word.

She was tempted to go after Tyrese, but she decided it would not be wise. It was better not to pry. Still, Zaire was bothered by his reaction.

"I thought you might be hungry," Tyrese said, holding up a bag of Thai food. "Max told me that this is your favorite. We're both working late, so I thought I'd grab some takeout."

She smiled. "It is and I am."

He sat down on the sofa beside her. "Zaire, I don't want you staying late too often. We've never had any incidents, but I want you to be careful. Make sure one of our security guards walks you to your car."

"I won't make it a habit. I promise."

Tyrese's eyes traveled around the room as they ate. "I meant to tell you that I really like what you've done in here."

Zaire wiped her mouth on the edge of her napkin. "I suppose you can tell that I love color."

He chuckled. "It tells me that you're not afraid to take chances."

She boldly met his gaze. "No, I'm not. Life is all about taking risks. We just have to be mindful of the ones we take. Regardless, we should learn lessons from the good and bad."

Her words both stunned and relieved him.

"You didn't do this by yourself," Zaire continued. "Like I told you earlier, I wanted to kiss you. I don't have any regrets."

"I don't want to risk our partnership," Tyrese stated. "I really believe that you, Pilar and I make a great team."

"I agree," she said. "However, I am mature enough to keep my personal and professional lives separate."

He did not respond.

"Tyrese, we're fine. There is no reason for you to worry. I'll see you tomorrow, partner."

"Good night."

"Good night," Zaire responded.

Tyrese could not discern any hidden meanings in her words. They were simple and straightforward.

It was not as easy for him to dismiss their kiss as Zaire had seemed to do. He wasn't sure how he felt about that.

"I like that," he responded.

Tyrese was so close she could feel the heat from his body. His closeness was so male, so bracing.

Their eyes met and held.

His eyes never strayed from her face. It felt as if he were kissing her with his eyes.

Zaire found the prolonged anticipation of the inevitable almost unbearable.

In one forward motion, she was in his arms.

Tyrese kissed her hungrily.

The caress of his lips on her mouth set her body aflame. Zaire wound her arms inside his jacket and around his back. Her body tingled from the contact.

She gave herself freely to the passion of his kiss.

Abruptly, Tyrese pulled away, leaving her mouth burning with fire.

"I'm sorry," he uttered. "I never should have done that."

"Tyrese, it's okay," Zaire quickly assured him. "I wanted you to kiss me."

He shook his head. "No, we can't do this."

"Why not?" Zaire demanded as she experienced an odd twinge of disappointment. His lips on hers had been divine ecstasy. Her emotions whirled and skidded to a stop. "Tyrese, you can't tell me that you're not attracted to me. I can see it in your face every time you look at me."

"Zaire, I make it a point to never get involved with anyone I work with."

Suddenly all pleasure left her. "Do you always have to play it so safe?"

"I didn't always," Tyrese admitted. "And when I didn't, there was a high price to pay. I can't go through that again."

"Will you be honest with me?"

He nodded.

"Do you have feelings for me?" Zaire asked.

"Yes," Tyrese answered. "I care more for you than I ever imagined possible."

"So you're saying that you will never act on those feelings," she said. "I am your partner, Tyrese. I find it hard to be so close to you and pretend that I don't care about you. Is it that easy for you?"

"No, it's not easy, but I know that this is what's best for us both in the long run."

Zaire shook her head. "I don't agree."

"I'm sorry." His expression was a mask of stone.

Tyrese strode briskly out of her office.

She ached with an inner pain.

He had feelings for her, but Tyrese would rather ignore them, leaving Zaire to believe that she would never fully understand men.

Tyrese sat in his living room in lonely silence, surrounded by darkness.

What was I thinking by kissing her? He was not one to let his emotions get the better of him. *So what happened?*

Zaire brought out feelings in him that Tyrese had

thought were long dead. He was shaken by what had taken place between them. He could not risk a repeat of what had happened in Chicago.

Tyrese knew exactly what he had to do—he had to stay as far away from Zaire as possible. At least until he could get his desires under control.

He decided that it was not wise for them to work late together, so when Zaire stayed late, Tyrese decided that he would have to leave. She was upset right now, but he was sure that Zaire would come around to his way of thinking. They both wanted their business partnership to flourish, so that should be their main focus.

Tyrese rose to his feet and navigated in the darkness to the stairs leading to the second floor of his home.

He walked into his bedroom and turned on a lamp

A thread of guilt snaked down his spine. He should have kissed Zaire like that. Tyrese c calling her, but he changed his mind. May to just pretend that it had never happe

Zaire did not seem like the vind could never really know when did not really know her.

Tyrese picked up the number.

"Hello."

"Zaire, I v tions."

"You don't have

"I'm not going to acc that's what you're worri

Chapter 7

The next day, Zaire smiled and nodded at Tyrese when they met in the hall as if nothing had happened. She was going to give him exactly what he wanted—space.

She did not miss the way he quirked his eyebrow in question but did not try to engage her in conversation. Zaire resisted the urge to look back at him, and she could feel the heat of his gaze on her.

She walked into her office, settled down at her desk and prepared to get her day started.

Tyrese must have walked by her office at least twenty times in the three hours she had been there.

Zaire couldn't resist a smile at the thought. He was having a hard time of it, just as she was; only she did not have to find reasons to leave her desk to snatch glimpses of Tyrese.

She set her chin in a stubborn line. Tyrese would have to come to her if he changed his mind about pursuing a relationship. Zaire would never give him another chance to reject her.

"Something's going on with Tyrese," Max said in a loud whisper as he entered her office. He sat down in a visitor chair, facing her. "He's acting all weird."

"I haven't noticed one way or the other," Zaire responded.

She looked up to see him pause just inside her door.

"Did you want me?" she asked, the double meaning evident.

A muscle quivered at his jaw. "I...I wanted to let you know that I've ordered lunch for everyone. It should arrive within the hour."

Zaire awarded him a huge smile. "That's so sweet, Tyrese. Thank you."

Max uttered a quick "Thank you," as well.

When he left, she found Max staring at her and grinning.

"What?"

"I... You and Tyrese..."

She shook her head. "My relationship with Tyrese is purely professional, Max."

"Yes, ma'am."

Zaire settled back in her plush leather chair. "Let's get back to work."

Zaire spent her Saturday looking for a new home.

"I really like this one," she told her mother after

they had looked at several apartment buildings within a ten-mile radius of M.G. Hill Creste was decidedly her favorite.

The moment she stepped into the two-bedroom apartment with hardwood flooring, granite counters and stainless-steel appliances, Zaire felt as if she had come home.

"It's close to M.G. and Beverly Hills. I really like the waterfalls in the pool area and outdoor fireplace."

"It is very nice," Barbara said.

Zaire broke into a grin. "This is going to be my new home, Mama."

"There is also a concierge business center, a media screening room and twenty-four-hour controlled access to our gated community," the leasing agent told Zaire.

"I love it," Zaire responded. "Let's get started on the paperwork."

She exhaled a long sigh of contentment. Her life was perfect. Except in the romance department.

Zaire tossed the thought away. For now, she wanted to focus on all the good things happening to her.

"Why don't we see if your daddy can join us for a little celebratory lunch?" Barbara suggested.

Zaire agreed, "Give him a call while I'm filling out my paperwork. We can meet him wherever you two decide. I'm open."

Her cell phone began to vibrate. Zaire hid her disappointment when she realized that it was not Tyrese.

He was avoiding her—she was pretty sure of it.

Zaire turned her attention once more to the paperwork on the desk in front of her.

* * *

She stayed after work on Monday to work out in the gym. Zaire heard someone come in but did not turn around.

She kept her focus on her workout. Normally, whenever she came, there were only one or two others in the gym with her. Most of the staff came early in the mornings or worked out during lunch.

Tyrese stepped on the treadmill next to her.

"I thought you were gone for the day," he said.

"Nope, I'm still here," she managed to reply through stiff lips.

They worked out in silence. In fact, Tyrese turned up the volume on the television to listen to the news, although Zaire believed that it was his way of avoiding a conversation with her.

Out of the corner of her eye, she saw him flexing his strong, muscled arms before increasing his pace.

Zaire struggled to keep her focus off Tyrese.

He was lean, toned and muscled in all of the right places. He looked good in his custom-made suits, but she couldn't deny that Tyrese looked incredibly sexy in sweatpants and a T-shirt.

Zaire managed to make it six miles on the treadmill before her cooldown.

Tyrese was still watching the news as he jogged.

She turned it off and walked over to stretch.

He came up behind her, placing a hand on her forearm.

Zaire turned around expectantly, brushing her hair away from her perspiration-damp forehead.

"You forgot your towel," Tyrese said. He stared with longing at her.

"Thank you." Tyrese remained standing there, gazing into her face.

It was Zaire who broke the look. "It's getting late. I should get out of here. My parents are expecting me for dinner."

He reached out, grabbing her hand.

Her heart pounded an erratic rhythm and her skin tingled from the contact.

"Zaire…"

"I'll see you in the morning," she said softly.

"I'll walk you to your car."

She shook her head. "I'll be fine, Tyrese. You don't have to worry about me."

Zaire walked to the doors and out of the gym, her heart racing. She felt a shred of disappointment when he did not bother to follow her.

Chapter 8

Zaire moved into her new apartment the following weekend. She couldn't have been happier. She and her siblings sat on the floor amid cardboard boxes, eating pizza.

"Thanks for all of your help," she told them.

"Nice digs," Drayden said as his eyes bounced around the room. "Very nice."

"This is almost as big as my condo," Blaze said, helping himself to another slice of spinach and mushroom pizza.

She laughed. "It's not even close."

"Livi and I have been looking at houses," Blaze announced. "I think we're going to find something near Marina del Rey."

"Are you two thinking of starting a family?" Zaire inquired.

He nodded. "We're both ready to have children."

Zaire glanced over at Drayden. "So have you found the woman you want to spend the rest of your life with?"

"No," he responded. "Not yet, but then, I have not been looking very hard. I've been concentrating on building my firm."

After they had eaten, Zaire told them, "Thanks again, guys. I can manage from here."

Blaze picked up his keys and headed to the door. "You don't have to tell me twice. I'm going home to spend some quality time with my wife."

Drayden put away the leftover pizza and then gathered up the cardboard boxes for the trash. "I'll take this outside."

"Thanks," she said with a grateful smile.

The doorbell sounded an hour later.

Zaire rose to her feet and crossed the room to look through the peephole.

She threw open the front door. "Tyrese..."

"I'm sorry for just dropping by without calling you.... I wanted..." He cleared his throat. "May I come in?"

Zaire stepped aside to let him enter. "I'm surprised to see you."

He handed her the plant he carried in both hands. "I wanted to get you something to celebrate your new place."

She took the plant from him. "Thank you. It's lovely. I have the perfect place for it."

Zaire set the plant near the window, and then she followed Tyrese into the living room. "I'm sorry, but the furniture won't be here until Thursday."

"It's fine," Tyrese assured her. "Zaire, I came to apologize again for the way I handled the night that I kissed you."

She watched with smug delight as he shifted uncomfortably.

"We just started our new partnership. I really don't want to mess it up by jumping into something we may not be ready for."

"You mean something that *you* are not ready for, Tyrese."

"Zaire…"

She held up her hand to halt whatever he was about to say. "If you want to keep our relationship a professional one—that's fine."

"I feel like there's a lot of tension between us right now."

"I just don't get you," she sputtered in frustration. "Tyrese, I have never met someone who was so rigid and reserved when it comes to feelings. Have you ever done anything really impulsive?"

Tyrese seemed a little taken aback by her question.

"Sometimes being impulsive can get you into trouble, Zaire."

"It's all good, Tyrese," she responded. "Our relaing to be engrossed in her work. She was not going to let him affect her to the point that she could not give her best when it came to work.

Putting all thoughts of Tyrese out of her mind helped tremendously. After her meetings, Zaire felt like celebrating.

She took Max out to lunch as a show of gratitude for all of his help.

"We did it," she told him. "I want you to know how much I really appreciate your help. Max, you and I make a great team. I'm looking forward to a long working relationship."

He smiled. "So am I. I really like working with you, Zaire. Hey, I noticed that Tyrese was sitting in the back of the conference room. Did you see him?"

Zaire was surprised. "Really?"

She'd had no idea that he had been present during er meetings. Zaire had been nervous and focused. e'd known Max was somewhere in the room, but couldn't remember seeing him.

aire finished off her lunch. "I guess we'd better ck to the office. We have to prepare for our last g for the day. Afterward, I'm going down to the work out. It's the perfect way to end a good but day."

of apprehension swept through Zaire as she arking deck. Biting her lip, she glanced lder several times but did not see anyone. eared normal; however, the tiny hairs r neck protested otherwise.

tionship is strictly professional from here on out, just as you wished."

"I would rather not risk ruining our partnership if things didn't work out between us."

Zaire shrugged nonchalantly. "It really doesn't matter."

"Yes, it does," he said. "I don't like this tension between us, Zaire."

"Then maybe you should leave," she suggested softly. "Tyrese, you and I are never going to agree on this subject."

"Maybe you're right." Tyrese watched her for a moment before heading to the door. He paused long enough to say, "I really hope that this won't impact our partnership."

"I wouldn't give you the satisfaction," Zaire uttered. "You will have to look at me every single day knowing that you lost out on the best thing to ever come into your life."

His eyes widened in surprise.

Zaire folded her arms across her chest. Her lips were pressed shut so no sound would burst out. She imposed an iron control on herself. Zaire refused to allow Tyrese to see her shed a tear over him.

He left her apartment.

She bit her lip to stifle the outcry and fought hard against the tears she refused to let fall.

Tyrese doesn't deserve me. He was definitely not the man Zaire had thought he was.

* * *

He felt like an idiot.

Tyrese had believed he was doing the right thing by Zaire, but now he wasn't so sure. There was no point in second-guessing himself. She didn't want anything to do with him.

He grudgingly admitted that Zaire was most likely right about her being the best thing to ever happen to him. She really was something special.

Tyrese considered giving Zaire a few days to deal with this without seeing him, but then he realized he was acting like a coward.

He enjoyed working with her and vowed to find a way to make this right. Over time, Zaire would come to realize that it was better this way in the long run. One day, she might even thank him.

The only problem with this theory was that Tyrese had trouble convincing his own heart. How in the world could he convince Zaire of something that he had not fully committed to? Tyrese drew a deep breath and exhaled slowly. He had hoped to prove to himself that he was immune to her, but he was failing miserably.

Pride kept him from calling Zaire.

He had to be strong and keep to his convictions. The incident in Chicago had taught him that, despite the vastly different circumstances. The only thing similar in both situations was that both women were connected to very powerful men—men that could destroy careers with a wave of the hand.

Tyrese had already experienced the wrath of one man who'd vowed to make sure he never saw the light of day because of a woman. He was never going to let that happen again.

"Good morning," Zaire greeted as she walked past Tyrese in the hallway. She didn't miss a step as she headed to her office.

She didn't linger to speak with him. He had already made up his mind, so there was nothing more to be said outside of anything pertaining to business.

Max was waiting in her office with a cup of tea for Zaire.

She smiled. "How did you know I would need th'

"I checked your calendar and thought you cou' some hot tea this morning."

Zaire met his gaze. "Oh, I forgot. I have back meetings this morning with two of M.G.'s ents. Max, what was I thinking?" She c ning to Tyrese for help, but with the them, Zaire stood her ground. Sh this on her own.

"I was thinking that we roc your tea, and I'll go set up room."

"Thanks."

Zaire sat dow puter.

She could hear office with a client.

Zaire averted her gaz

She had never stayed this late before and had not intended to do so now. Time had slipped by during her workout. Zaire decided that, going forward, she would not do it again unless there were others working in the office, as well.

Zaire was suddenly anxious to escape the empty parking deck. She became increasingly uneasy.

She had never felt so uncomfortable out alone like this.

Zaire heard what sounded like footsteps and quickened her pace.

It was probably security, she told herself. She shouldn't be worried, but the warning voice in her head could still be heard.

This time the sound of footsteps echoed louder, sending a thread of fear through Zaire and alarm bells ringing. She walked faster, her keys in hand. She could press the panic button if necessary, but surprisingly, this did nothing to end the disquieting thoughts running rampant in her mind.

Zaire released a sigh of relief when she was within yards of her car. In a matter of minutes, she would be in it and driving away to the safety of her home.

Suddenly a man appeared in front of her.

Zaire screamed before everything went black.

Tyrese answered his cell phone on the second ring. "Hello."

"Mr. Moore, I think you'd better come to the office," one of his security personnel stated. "There's been an incident."

Tyrese immediately picked up his car keys and headed toward the door. "What happened?" he stammered.

"Miss Alexander," the security guard began. "Someone attacked her. They wanted her car."

"I'll be right there."

The police had arrived and so had the ambulance by the time he pulled up. Tyrese parked his car right nearby. He shifted the gear to Park and then rushed over to check on Zaire. The police wouldn't let him near her.

The paramedics were placing an unconscious Zaire on a stretcher.

"How is she?"

"You are?" one of the policemen asked.

"Tyrese Moore," he answered thickly. "I am the owner of this building. How is Zaire?"

"From the looks of it, someone punched her in the face. She may have been hit or kicked. There's a red BMW crashed in the parking garage."

"It's her car," Tyrese confirmed.

"This was a carjacking," the police stated. "The perp got away, unfortunately. She's going to be taken to Cedars-Sinai Hospital."

"She's my partner. I'm going with her."

Tyrese climbed into the ambulance. He took her slender hand in his. "I'm right here," he whispered. "You're safe now."

He swallowed hard, trying to keep his fear at bay. Tyrese wanted her to open her eyes. She looked pale and it bothered him to see her so still.

The police had found her wallet somewhere in the car. They were not very forthcoming with details at the moment. Her red tote was also still in the car with the laptop. He had overheard this much. Apparently, the person who'd attacked Zaire had been in such a hurry that he'd never noticed the tote.

Tyrese played a number of scenarios in his head. He knew that it was Zaire's usual routine to take her tote to the car before working out. Apparently, the person who'd attacked her was an amateur, and for that, he was grateful. The situation could have turned out much worse.

He waited until they had arrived at the hospital and Zaire had been taken to one of the emergency rooms before calling her parents.

"Mr. Alexander, this is Tyrese Moore. Zaire was attacked and she's at Cedars-Sinai. I'm here with her."

"Her mother and I will be right there."

Tyrese was surprised at how calm Malcolm had sounded over the phone. He saw a nurse coming out of the room that Zaire was in. He rushed over to her.

"Is she awake?"

"She was awake for a moment," the woman responded. "Miss Alexander was in a lot of pain so we gave her something to help. She's sleeping, but she will be fine."

Tyrese prayed she was right.

Chapter 9

Ari Alexander was the first one in Zaire's family to arrive at the hospital. Tyrese recognized him and crossed the room to meet him. "I just spoke with the doctor. Zaire was hit in the face and has a broken tooth, but she will be fine."

"What happened exactly?" Ari asked.

"She was attacked in the M.G. employee parking deck. Someone tried to steal her car."

A young woman who was obviously pregnant and a man approached them. "Where is Zaire?"

"Sage, you shouldn't have come," Ari told her. "You don't need to get yourself all upset. You have a baby to consider."

"My sister was attacked," she snapped. "I'm going

to be upset no matter where I am. I'm going to be here in case Zaire needs me."

Sage glanced over at Tyrese and asked, "Where were you when this all happened?"

"I wasn't there," he explained. "I am going to do everything in my power to get to the bottom of this."

"I would have assumed that you would have security cameras everywhere," Ari muttered.

"I do," Tyrese said, his gaze steady. "I will be evaluating my security needs because of what's happened."

Malcolm and Barbara arrived with another man.

"You must be Tyrese Moore," Malcolm stated, walking up to Tyrese. "This is my wife, Barbara, and this is Franklin, my head of security."

"We'd like to keep this quiet," Barbara told him. "My daughter would not want this flashed across the tabloids."

He nodded in understanding. "I've already spoken to the medical staff about that."

"I'm going to talk to them, as well," Malcolm said. "I want to make sure they understand that this is not to get out in any form or fashion. My daughter's tragedy will not be plastered all over the world and the internet."

"I am going to stay here to make sure no one takes any photographs," Franklin announced. "Only the medical team will be allowed in the room, and I intend to make sure they do not bring in their cell phones."

Men like Malcolm had the power to keep certain things out of the news, make or break careers and even ruin reputations, Tyrese thought with light bitterness.

He had no doubt that Malcolm would destroy the person responsible for leaking the news of Zaire's attack.

Tyrese was a powerful man within his own right, but he had never been the type of person hungry to avenge the wrongs done to him—not to the point of destroying a person. It was just not his way.

Ari approached him. "Thank you for all you've done, Tyrese. We can handle it from here."

He did not want to leave without seeing Zaire, but Ari's tone brooked no argument.

"I'll tell her you were here."

Tyrese gave a slight nod and then turned to leave. He took a taxi back to the office. He checked in with security as soon as he arrived.

His mood veered to anger. "I can't believe we have all of this high-tech equipment and yet we could not get one clear image of the person who attacked Zaire."

"Mr. Moore—"

"I don't want this situation to ever happen again. If we need more cameras installed, then see to it."

He couldn't get Zaire out of his thoughts. Tyrese stayed with the family at the hospital until he was sure she was going to be fine.

The image of Zaire's bruised face haunted him.

Tyrese curled his hands into fists. She didn't deserve to be punched in the face like that—no one did.

He called the hospital before heading home, but her family had requested that no calls be put through to the room. They wanted her to get some rest.

Tyrese groaned in frustration.

* * *

Zaire opened her eyes and then closed them quickly to block out the blinding-bright lights. She heard her parents' voices and lifted her head.

"She's awake, Mama."

She recognized Sage's voice and whispered, "What are you doing here? You should be home resting."

"I'll go home when I know that you are going to be fine."

"I hurt, but I'll be okay." Zaire tried to sit up, but she was still shaky.

Barbara took the remote and raised the bed for her. "Honey, I'm so glad to see those beautiful eyes of yours."

She put a hand to her still-swollen mouth. "My…"

Her mother placed a gentle hand to her cheek. "Shh… dear. It's going to be all right."

"I look a mess."

Malcolm sat down on the edge of the hospital bed. "You're still beautiful."

"Tyrese…"

"He was here," Barbara said. "He rode in the ambulance with you. He would probably still be here, but Ari sent him home."

"Why did he do that?" Zaire wanted to know.

"He thought Tyrese's presence would prompt too many questions," her father responded. "The doctor said you can come home with us. Tyrese can visit you there."

"Do you have a mirror?" she asked Sage.

"I don't," her sister responded.

Zaire moved to get out of bed. "I need to see how bad I look."

"Honey, don't..." her mother pleaded.

"I have to do this." Zaire placed a hand on her stomach. The guy who had attacked her had kicked her, too. Her ribs were bruised, but had not been broken.

She walked slowly to the bathroom.

Her father tried to assist her, but she refused his help. "I can do this, Daddy."

Zaire winced as she eyed her reflection in the mirror. Her face had a bruise, her lip was cut and her tooth had been chipped. Her eyes filled with tears.

She put a fist to her mouth to stifle her sobs. Why had this happened to her? Zaire had never done anything to hurt another person, so why did some stranger want to hurt her like this? He had been vicious in his attack.

Zaire feared he had stolen her wallet and knew where she lived. She was afraid to go home. She would not feel safe until she knew that her attacker was behind bars.

Barbara knocked on the bathroom door. "Honey, are you okay?"

"I'm fine," she answered. "I'll be right out."

Deep down, Zaire did not believe that anything would ever be right again. Her life was forever changed.

Zaire slept all of the way home due to the pain medication she was taking.

Her mother woke her gently. "We're home, sweetie."

Malcolm helped her out of the car and escorted her upstairs to her bedroom. Barbara followed close behind.

Zaire turned the doorknob slowly, opening the door wide to reveal a rich purple-and-gold color scheme throughout.

"I'm glad you decided to come home with us," her mother said.

"Me, too," Zaire managed to say. Although her wallet had been found in her car, Zaire still feared that her attacker might show up at her apartment.

She walked over to the bed, running her fingers along the delicate etchings of the mahogany bed.

"Honey, do you need anything?"

Zaire looked over her shoulder at her mother. "No, ma'am. I just want to lie down for a while."

She crossed the gleaming hardwood floor, heading to the eight-drawer chest. Zaire retrieved a pair of knit shorts and a T-shirt.

"I'm going to take a shower."

Her parents exchanged looks but said nothing.

"I'm fine," Zaire said, trying to reassure them.

"I'll check on you in a while," Barbara told her.

She nodded but did not speak.

Zaire slipped out of her shoes and padded barefoot into the bathroom. She turned on the shower, undressed and stepped inside, letting the warm temperature of the water soothe her sore body.

Tears filled her eyes and rolled down her cheeks.

Zaire put a fist up to her mouth to smother her sobs. She had never known such fear in her life. She was grateful that the man had only tried to steal her car—the situation could have turned out much worse. Still, Zaire could not escape the memories that haunted her dreams.

When the sobs subsided, Zaire turned off the shower. She dried off and slipped on the shorts and T-shirt.

Zaire opened the bathroom door and peeked out.

She was relieved to find that her parents were gone. Zaire did not feel like talking or having company. She just wanted to be alone.

Zaire pulled down the covers on her king-size bed and climbed in.

She just wanted to sleep.

Zaire did not know whether it was the effects of the medication or what she had gone through—it did not matter as long as she could close her eyes.

She was vaguely aware of her mother slipping into the room later, closing the curtains and casting the room in darkness.

Chapter 10

It was driving him nuts to the point that Tyrese could not wait any longer. He had to see Zaire, so he left work and drove the thirty minutes it took to get to Pacific Palisades. He had placed a call earlier to Malcolm to obtain permission to come to the house.

"How is she?" Tyrese asked as soon as he arrived.

"As well as can be expected," Malcolm responded. "She had a nightmare last night."

"I've made some changes to ensure that this will never happen again. We've installed additional surveillance cameras around the building and more in the parking deck."

"I'm glad to hear it," Malcolm stated. "Hopefully, there won't be another occurrence. This incident has forced me to review the security at all of our properties."

"I'd like to see Zaire, if it's all right with you," Tyrese announced.

Malcolm eyed him for a moment before replying, "I'm not sure she's up for company, but I'll check."

"Thank you."

Tyrese waited in the living room for Malcolm to return. He couldn't wait to lay eyes on Zaire. She had plagued his thoughts since the attack, and he just needed to see her for himself.

"I didn't realize we had company," Barbara said as she descended the stairs. "How are you, Tyrese?"

"I'm fine," he responded. "I came by to see Zaire."

She smiled. "I gathered as much."

Malcolm returned. "Zaire would like you to come up to her room. I'll take you up there."

He knocked on the door and waited for her invitation to enter.

"Come in."

Tyrese opened the door and stepped inside to find Zaire lying beneath a throw on the chaise in her bedroom. Her face was still swollen, and her bruises were turning colors. She looked away when he approached her.

"I hope you don't mind that I'm here. Zaire, I really needed to see you for myself. I've been going crazy since you got hurt."

"I'm fine," she mumbled. Her tooth had been chipped in the front, and it was clear that she was self-conscious about her appearance.

"I'm so sorry this happened to you," he whispered. Tyrese sat down on the edge of the chaise.

She put a hand over her mouth as she talked. "It's not your fault, Tyrese. You warned me about staying too late in the evenings. I should have listened to you."

Her voice was barely above a whisper, forcing Tyrese to strain to hear her.

Tyrese rose to his feet.

He sat down beside her on the chaise, and then he reached over to gently pull her hand away from her face. "You are still a very beautiful woman, Zaire. You don't have to hide from me."

Her gray eyes filled with tears. "He broke my tooth, and he punched me in the face. He kicked me in the stomach."

Tyrese embraced her, hoping to comfort her. He hated seeing her in so much pain. "It's going to be all right. I will never allow something like this to happen ever again."

"I was so scared."

Tyrese nodded in understanding.

"If all he wanted was the car...all he had to do was ask. He didn't have to hit me. Why are people so cruel?"

There was a knock on the door, and then Barbara stuck her head inside. "It's time for us to leave, dear."

Tyrese glanced at Zaire, who said, "I have an appointment with my dentist. He's going to repair my tooth."

He hid his disappointment. Tyrese had hoped to spend some time with her that afternoon, but he also understood the reason for the rush to get her tooth repaired. He would respond in the same manner had he been in her shoes.

"Do you want to go with us?" she asked him.

"No, I'll give you a call later. Maybe I can come back to visit you tomorrow, if you're up for it."

"I'd like that, Tyrese."

He escorted her down the stairs, where her parents were waiting for them.

Malcolm opened the front door.

Zaire took a tentative step toward it and then stopped. She clutched her chest. "I can't breathe," she said between rapid panting.

"She's hyperventilating," Tyrese stated. "Zaire needs to sit down."

Her mother reached out to rub her back.

"No, don't touch me," she snapped. "Please…I can't breathe."

"She's having a panic attack," Tyrese said.

Barbara looked almost as stricken as Zaire.

"I can't do it," Zaire said, tears rolling down her cheeks. "I can't go."

Tyrese glimpsed the fear in her eyes. "It's okay, sweetheart," he whispered. "Right now, I just want you to close your eyes and visualize your favorite place in the world. Close your eyes."

She did as she was told.

"Slow down your breathing," he said softly. "That's it. You're doing well."

Zaire appeared much calmer a few minutes later.

"Honey, do you want me to cancel the appointment?" Barbara asked.

"No," she responded. "I need to get my tooth fixed. Can't he come here to the house?"

Tyrese reached over and took her hand. "Zaire, you can do this."

She shook her head. "I can't. Just the thought of leaving this house... I can't breathe. I feel like I'm dying." Zaire wiped away a tear.

"I won't leave your side," he assured her. "You trust me, don't you?"

She nodded.

"Just hold on to me," he whispered. "I want you to close your eyes. Keep them closed until I tell you to open them."

Zaire gasped when Tyrese picked her up. She held on to him for dear life when she felt the cool air against her skin.

Her chest began to tighten, and it was increasingly hard for Zaire to breathe.

Tyrese must have sensed her distress because he whispered, "Inhale slowly...good. Now exhale..."

Zaire had no idea whose car she was in, but it did not feel familiar. She considered that it was Tyrese's until she heard her father talking. She kept her eyes closed and she concentrated on breathing.

"You're doing so well, dear."

"Mama..."

"I'm here with you, sweetie. Your daddy and I are right here with you."

Zaire leaned against Tyrese for strength. She inhaled the light, woodsy scent of his cologne. Her head fitted perfectly in the hollow between his shoulder and neck. She relaxed, sinking into his cushioning embrace.

Tyrese must have sensed her need for silence because he did not attempt to draw her into conversation. He gently massaged her arm as she clung to him.

Zaire had calmed down when they arrived at the medical building where the dental office was housed. She was able to get out of the car and walk without assistance into the waiting room.

Tyrese sat down beside her. "You're doing great," he told her in a low voice.

When her name was called, Zaire insisted on going back on her own. However, she felt the onset of panic once again when the dentist came into the room they had placed her in.

"Miss Alexander, how are you?"

Zaire's body trembled, affecting her words. "F-fine. J-just want to get this over w-with."

"Your mother explained what happened. We can sedate you if that will make you feel more comfortable."

Zaire nodded. "That's what I want," she replied. "It's the only way I'll be able to get through the procedure."

An hour and a half later, they were heading back to Pacific Palisades. She was still groggy from the sedation, which made the trip back to the house easier for her to bear.

some time to work through it. Zaire, take as much time as you need. Working from home may be just what you need right now. Eventually, you'll be able to come back to the office."

"I didn't feel safe when we left the house yesterday even though you and my parents were with me. Tyrese, I'm not sure I will ever feel safe again."

"Zaire, you will get through this, and you don't have to do it alone. You have your family...and you have me."

"I appreciate you saying that, Tyrese."

"I mean it. I am going to be by your side every step of the way."

"I hope that you won't come to regret that."

"I won't," he said. "I have a meeting later this evening, but I'd like to spend some time with you tomorrow, if it's okay with you."

"I'd really like that. I look forward to your visits."

"Same here," he murmured.

After they hung up, Tyrese typed the word *agorapho-*into Google. He wanted to learn everything about condition, but he especially wanted to research treat-ptions.

dened him to see Zaire a reflection of her for-She lived in constant fear. Her mother had th him that since the attack a few days ago, her bedroom windows locked; she was not ven sitting on the patio. She did not like me alone. If Barbara and Malcolm were would stay in the house with her.

been repaired, but Zaire wanted to sell

* * *

Tyrese was grateful when Barbara invited him to stay for lunch. Zaire had gone back to her room. He had stayed with her until she'd fallen asleep.

"I really appreciate your help with Zaire," Barbara told him. "It's hard for me because she's never been afraid of anything. I guess we sheltered her too much."

"She believes there's good in everybody," Tyrese said. "It's not a bad thing, but it may take her some time to get past the reality that there are some horrible people in the world and they don't care who they hurt."

"You sound as if you speak from experience," Malcolm commented.

Tyrese leaned back in his chair. "I do."

Barbara wiped her mouth with the corner of her napkin. "I just hope she will find the strength to get past this. She has the rest of her life to live, and I don't want her to do it in fear."

Malcolm nodded in agreement.

"I believe that Zaire should consider therapy at some point," Tyrese said. "If she doesn't, she may not ever leave this house again. The way she responded today seems similar to agoraphobia."

Barbara looked stricken. "Oh, I hope that it doesn't come to that."

"I hope you don't mind my asking," Malcolm began. "How do you know so much about this condition?"

"A friend of mine developed it after 9/11," Tyrese explained. "He's still unable to work and is on full disability."

"Is he able to leave his home?"

"No."

Barbara's eyes teared up. "I'm so sorry to hear that." She glanced over at her husband. "I suppose we need to keep a watch on Zaire."

Malcolm agreed.

Shortly after four o'clock, Tyrese left the Alexander estate despite his deepest desire to stay with Zaire. He would have preferred to be there when she woke up, but he did not want to wear out his welcome.

All Tyrese wanted to do was protect Zaire from further harm.

Chapter 11

"Thanks so much for your help yeste Tyrese when she called him the next think I could have made it to the d you. I don't know what happer of leaving home... I had a p

"How are you feeling t

"Better than yesterd She paused a momer reason I called is to ing to the office

She placed ing the ho anxious."

"You've been t Tyrese responded.

it. She said it reminded her of what had happened when she wanted nothing more than to forget.

"Is there something going on between you and Tyrese?" Barbara asked when Zaire put her cell phone down on the breakfast counter.

Zaire glanced over at her mother. "Why would you ask me that?"

"He seems to care a great deal about you."

"He is a really nice guy, Mama," she said. "When his assistant's babysitter did not show up, he told her to bring the baby to work. He set up an empty office as a temporary nursery. Tyrese is always doing things like that. Max told me that when one of his staff couldn't get to work because his car kept breaking down, he advanced the guy enough money for a down payment on a better one."

"That was a wonderful gesture," Barbara said as she handed Zaire a cup of hot tea. "But I'm not convinced he doesn't have stronger feelings where you are concerned."

Zaire took a sip of her tea. "How do you feel about it?"

Barbara shrugged. "I don't want to see you get hurt, Zaire. Office romances are not a good idea, but they do happen. The only thing I would say is that you have to be able to separate your business relationship from a personal one."

"He's my partner, Mama. We have to get to know each other."

Barbara let the subject drop. Instead, she questioned, "Honey, how are you really feeling?"

"There are times when I relive what happened and then I feel like I can't breathe. I've been having panic attacks. The mere thought of leaving home brings them on, as well. Mama, there's something really wrong with me."

"Would you be willing to see a therapist?" Barbara asked.

"I don't know."

"There's nothing wrong with seeing help. You don't want to become a prisoner in this house, dear."

"I can't talk about this right now, Mama," she said.

"Okay, we can change the subject."

Zaire stepped out of her chair and walked over to the French doors. She stared outside, past the patio toward the ocean. She missed the way the water felt on her bare feet when she strolled along the beach.

She craved the feel of the ocean air on her skin. Zaire's eyes traveled the length of the pool.

Zaire could still remember the day she'd entered this house for the very first time. What excited her most about the home were the pool and the view. She loved the outdoors, which was why this felt like a death sentence to her. Zaire wanted to try to work through her fears on her own, but she did not seem to be getting any better. She still had nightmares. Zaire knew that her fear was irrational, but she could not get it under control. She was fine as long as she was home.

* * *

"Tyrese, why don't you ever talk about yourself?" Zaire inquired as they settled in the family room to watch television. They had just finished eating dinner ordered from a nearby restaurant. Her parents had previously committed to attending an event. Tyrese had volunteered to stay with Zaire until they returned.

He met her gaze. "There is nothing interesting about me to talk about."

"I don't believe that. Everybody has a story. Why don't we start with where you are from?" Zaire asked. "I know it's not Los Angeles."

Tyrese eyed her with amusement. "I'm from Chicago."

"What brought you out here?"

"You're not going to let this go, are you?"

Grinning, she shook her head. "I want to know more about my partner."

"I would rather hear about you," Tyrese said. He picked up a photo album. "What were you like as a child?"

"You'd better not open that book unless you are prepared to show me photographs from your childhood."

"I don't have any," he said quietly. "When I was ten, we had a house fire and we lost everything."

"I'm sorry."

"You had no way of knowing."

"How did it happen?"

"I didn't know a whole lot about it at the time, but I later learned that some people wanted my dad to sell and he refused. Then the fire happened and they said it was arson, but they accused him of setting the fire. I don't think the insurance paid because of that. We ended up moving in with my grandparents. That's when I met Pilar."

"So they never found the person responsible?"

Tyrese shook his head. "The person my parents believed had the house burned down was a very wealthy man who owned lots of real estate—he made millions selling it off to developers. He died the year I graduated from high school. Someone shot him in the head and stuffed him in the trunk of his Mercedes."

"I guess somebody got tired of his antics and decided to make him pay."

"I guess so," Tyrese responded. "There are some men who wield their millions like power, and they don't care who they hurt. They develop a god complex over others."

Zaire agreed, "Eventually, they will find themselves on the receiving end of all they've done to hurt others. I believe that what goes around will come around."

Tyrese gave a short chuckle. "I used to believe that."

"Pilar is a beautiful and intelligent woman," Zaire said. "Did you two ever...?"

He shook his head. "She's like a sister to me."

"Are your parents still in Chicago?"

"My dad died when I was thirteen, and my mother died a year after I graduated high school. My grandparents died within months of each other after I graduated college."

"You've had a time of it, haven't you?"

"Actually, I had a good life for the most part," Tyrese explained. "I had parents and grandparents who loved me unconditionally. We didn't have much, but we had love."

Zaire smiled. "That's what is most important."

"I agree," Tyrese said.

She rose to her feet and walked over to the window. Zaire stared out at the ocean. "It's so pretty out here at night."

Tyrese moved to stand beside her. "You miss it, don't you? Being out there, savoring the feel of the night air on your face."

"I miss the way that I used to be. On a night like this, I would be right out there on the patio. I am tired of living this way, Tyrese. I feel trapped."

He leaned over and whispered, "One day soon, this will be a distant memory." Tyrese wrapped his arm around her waist.

She glanced up at him. "I hope that you're right, Tyrese."

Zaire felt the heat of desire wash over her like waves.

Turning her around so that she faced him, Tyrese leaned over and kissed her softly on the lips. "I've wanted to do that all night."

In response, Zaire pulled his head down to hers. Their lips met, and she felt buffeted by the winds of a savage harmony. Her senses reeled as if they'd short-circuited, and it made her knees tremble.

Breaking their kiss, Zaire buried her face against

his throat, her trembling limbs clung to him helplessly. She was extremely conscious of where Tyrese's warm flesh touched hers.

"You've saved my life in so many ways," she told him. "I will always be grateful for that."

"You've saved my life, too," Tyrese told her. "You and your family have shown me that there are still some really good people in the world. It's not about power and control with you all."

"One of the things my father made clear when he found out about his inheritance was that we were not going to let money change us in any way. He views his wealth as a means to help others less fortunate."

"This is as it should be," Tyrese responded.

His cell phone rang.

He glanced at it and turned it off.

"You don't need to do that," Zaire said with a smile. "If you need some privacy, feel free to use my father's office."

Tyrese shook his head. "That's not a call I need to return."

Zaire studied his expression. She thought she detected a flash of anger.

"Are you okay?" she asked.

He pasted on a smile. "I'm fine."

Picking up the remote, Tyrese inquired, "Have you decided on what you want to watch? Ladies' choice."

Zaire laughed. "You may come to regret that decision."

* * *

Zaire agreed to meet with a therapist a couple of days later. She was willing to try anything that would help her resume her normal life. Her parents located one willing to travel to Pacific Palisades. She was downstairs in the foyer when the woman arrived.

They settled in her father's office to talk.

"The goal of treatment is to help you free yourself from fear and return to a functional lifestyle," her therapist stated.

"I'd like that," Zaire said. "I just don't want to take medication."

"You can be treated without meds, but I have to warn you, Zaire, that it will be much more difficult."

"If I find that I need the medication, then I'll take it."

Her therapist nodded in approval.

"There are a variety of treatments available for agoraphobia, including psychotherapy."

"How does that work?" Zaire inquired.

"Cognitive behavioral therapy focuses on decreasing anxiety-provoking thoughts and behaviors. This form of psychotherapy has shown to be highly effective in treating agoraphobia."

"This is what I'd like to try."

"Cognitive behavioral therapy involves anywhere from ten to twenty sessions over a number of weeks. I will help you gain understanding and control of the stressful events or situations in your life. You will learn stress management and relaxation techniques. Finally, we will work from the least fearful to the most fearful, which is leaving this house."

Zaire met her gaze. "When can we get started? Living in fear is a horrible way to live."

When her session ended, she walked to the kitchen, where Barbara was preparing dinner.

"Where's Daddy?"

"He's in one of the guesthouses with Franklin," Barbara replied. "They are going over something with the hotel in Phoenix. There have been a couple of robberies."

"That's awful. I don't know why some people feel they have the right to steal what others have worked for," Zaire huffed.

"Franklin's flying there later tonight. He believes that it may have been an inside job. Your father may go with him."

"I hope that Daddy will press charges if it is one of the employees. They deserve to go to jail."

"How did things go with Dr. Graham?" Barbara asked.

"I like her," Zaire answered. "I made it clear that I did not want to be on meds."

Barbara pulled a pan of chicken from the oven. "I hope you're hungry. I made your favorite."

"Garlic roasted chicken," Zaire said with a smile. "I'm starved."

She helped her mother finish cooking.

Zaire was looking forward to her treatment for agoraphobia. She had always been one to come and go as she pleased. Being a prisoner in her parents' home brought on bouts of depression.

Then there was Tyrese, as well. They were becoming closer and closer, but Zaire was pretty sure he would grow bored of coming to the house all the time. They were never truly alone because her parents were always somewhere in the house.

Zaire was not going to stay a victim. She was determined to get her life back.

Chapter 12

As soon as her therapy session ended, Zaire went to her room and picked up her iPad. She opened up Face-Time and clicked on Max's name.

"I just emailed you a list of local-area fitness trainers for Bill Daniels's retreat," he told her.

Zaire grinned. "Thanks! I don't know what I'd do without you."

"Hopefully, you never have to find out."

She laughed. "I'm expecting some contracts to arrive today. Can you please give them to Tyrese to bring to me?"

"Sure."

"Has Bill sent us his list of workshops?"

Max shook his head. "I can shoot him a quick email to remind him."

"Oh, make sure the trainers submit proposals that provide at least twenty hours of cardiovascular, flexibility and circuit training. They should also note if they are willing to provide personalized instruction for all levels to the attendees."

"There should be a daily therapeutic massage," Max suggested. "I'd certainly be ready for one after a day of fun and fitness training."

"See what packages they offer at the ranch. Maybe we can get an all-inclusive package for Daniels Auto."

Zaire ended her conversation with Max a few minutes later. She then focused her attention on an upcoming event for the Springhill Wine Company. The owner was a die-hard blues and rock and roll fan, so she negotiated for the Blues Brothers to perform at the launch party.

She did not leave her bedroom until well after six o'clock in the evening. Zaire went downstairs to start dinner. Her mother wasn't feeling well and had spent most of her day in her bedroom.

Zaire made a dinner salad.

She heard the front door open and went to see who it was. Zaire released the breath she was holding when she saw Ryan, her brother-in-law.

"Sage told me that your mother isn't feeling well. I made her some of my homemade chicken soup."

She smiled. "You have great timing, Ryan. I just made a salad and I was about to open up a can of soup, but this is so much better. Thanks a lot."

"When will your dad be back in town?" he asked.

"He and Franklin will be back on Friday," Zaire responded. "The investigation is taking longer than he originally thought."

Ryan met her gaze. "How are you doing?"

"Much better," she responded. "I've just started therapy."

"Good for you."

They talked for a few minutes before Ryan said, "Well, I'd better head back home. Sage wants to do a few laps in the pool. I don't want her in there unless I'm home with her."

"That's really sweet. I love how you are so protective of my sister."

"Sage is my life."

Zaire's deepest wish was to hear those words come out of Tyrese's mouth one day. She had fallen deeply in love with him. There was no other man for her.

"Max gave me this stuff to give to you," Tyrese announced upon his arrival. "I assume you were expecting it."

Zaire glanced up at him and smiled. "I was. I asked him to give it to you."

"I'm really glad to see you working like this. You seem like your old self."

"I'm not quite there yet," Zaire stated as she took the packet out of Tyrese's hands. "But I am working hard to get back to being me. I especially want to be able to leave this house. I can't just do all of my presentations via Skype, FaceTime or webinars."

He laughed. "From what I'm hearing, you are doing a great job and the presentations have been on point."

"Do you feel up to bowling?" Zaire asked.

Her parents loved bowling and they'd had a miniature bowling alley built when they had renovated the house.

"You bowl?" Tyrese asked.

"Why do you sound so surprised?" she asked, her hands on her hips.

He shrugged. "It just didn't seem like it would be your thing."

"We used to go bowling with my parents all of the time."

Tyrese broke into a grin. "So is that your way of telling me that you have skills?"

"I'll let my game do the talking."

They took the steps down to the basement.

Zaire let Tyrese choose his ball first, and then she chose hers.

She turned and looked up at him. "I want you to know that I play to win."

Tyrese watched Zaire as she pushed the ball straight out until her arms were fully extended. Her right hand supported the ball underneath. She looked as if she knew what she was doing, he decided.

His eyes traveled from the back of her head downward to the curve of her hips. Tyrese forced his eyes back to the game.

Zaire released the ball, rolling a perfect strike. "Yessss."

It was his turn.

When Tyrese saw the two pins left standing, he groaned.

"It's okay, baby," Zaire murmured. "You can knock them down."

"I appreciate the faith you have in me."

She kissed him on the cheek. "I have a lot of faith in you."

Tyrese met her gaze.

He placed the bowling ball on the rack before drawing Zaire into an embrace.

Tyrese pressed his lips against hers and then gently covered her mouth.

Zaire drank in the sweetness of his kisses.

He kissed the top of her nose, then her eyes and, finally, he returned his attention to her mouth. Zaire's lips were warm and sweet.

"I can't fight what I feel for you," he whispered. "I can't…"

Zaire took a step backward. "What exactly are you saying?" She looked as if she was trying to read his expression.

"Honey, I'm crazy about you. The night they called me about the attack…I felt as if a part of my heart…" Tyrese shook his head. "I was afraid that I would lose you. I don't think I've ever been so scared."

"I'm in love with you, Tyrese."

He met her gaze. "And I'm in love with you."

"So what do we do about it?" she asked.

"I wish I knew," Tyrese responded. "Zaire, there is a lot to consider here."

"What happened before?" Zaire questioned. "Did you get involved with someone from work in the past? It must have turned out badly for you to be so torn about this."

"She didn't work with me," Tyrese answered. "We dated for almost a year, and I was on the verge of asking her to marry me. The day that I was going to pick up her engagement ring, my boss called me into his office. He showed me photos of myself and his fiancée."

Zaire gasped in surprise. "She was engaged to your boss?"

Tyrese nodded. "I had no idea. She was a flight attendant and I figured when she wasn't with me, she was working. I really thought that what we had was something special."

"Is that why you left Chicago?"

"I had no other choice. She accused me of forcing my attentions on her, and my boss apparently believed her. I was fired. My old employer was very rich, and, because of his connections, I was blackballed and could not get a job anywhere in Illinois. Pilar invited me to come to Los Angeles and stay with her until I could get some things figured out. M.G. was birthed in her kitchen one night during dinner. I maxed out my credit cards and wiped out my savings to start the company. Thankfully, it paid off."

"I'm sorry you had to go through something like that."

"It was an important lesson learned."

"Do you still have feelings for this woman?" Zaire wanted to know.

Tyrese shook his head. "At one point, I despised her for the way she ruined my life, but not anymore. I don't feel anything for her, good or bad. There's nothing left."

"You don't want to get involved with me because you're afraid that I might use this as a way to ruin you, especially because my parents are rich."

"Yes," Tyrese admitted.

"We love each other, but we can't be together," Zaire uttered. "This just doesn't make sense to me."

"Zaire, we can sort this out later. Right now, you should be focusing on getting stronger."

She nodded. "You're right. I need to find a way to get better. I want so much to feel normal."

Tyrese embraced her. "I'm not going anywhere. I want you to know that."

"Please don't say things like that," she whispered. "It only makes me love you that much more."

Two days later, a dozen platinum-dipped roses arrived for Zaire.

"Looks like you and Tyrese are becoming very close," Malcolm stated. "Is there something I should know?"

"They are just flowers, Daddy," she said with a grin. "He knows that I love roses."

"Those are not *just flowers*," Malcolm countered. "These flowers cost at least a thousand dollars."

Zaire read the card that came with them.

Zaire, I chose to give you roses because I know how much you love them and because they represent my feelings for you. Both the roses and my love for you will last a lifetime.
Tyrese

She glanced over at Malcolm and tried to read his expression. "Daddy…"

"You're in love with this man."

"I am," Zaire confessed. "I know he's my partner and that it's not wise to mix business and pleasure, but, Daddy, I never expected this to happen. I love him so much."

Malcolm folded his arms across his chest. "Apparently he feels the same way about you."

She nodded. "Yes, but we haven't really acted on our feelings."

"What do you plan to do?"

"I don't know, Daddy. Tyrese doesn't want to ruin our partnership by getting involved with me and then it doesn't work out."

"I think it's a wise decision."

"Daddy, I love him and he loves me. I can't explain it, but I know that he is the man for me. We belong together like Mickey Mouse and Minnie, Scarlett O'Hara and Rhett Butler…you and Mama."

Malcolm smiled. "A man that sends you roses dipped in platinum is not ready to walk away, sweetie."

Zaire smiled. "Do we have your blessing?"

"He seems like a nice young man, and it's obvious that he cares deeply for you. You have my blessing."

She embraced her father. "Thank you, Daddy."

Chapter 13

Tyrese was becoming a regular visitor at the Alexander estate. Zaire looked forward to his visits with the anticipation of a child waiting for Santa Claus.

This was the first time he would be there for one of the Alexander cookouts. It had rained early, but did not last long.

"I'm so glad it stopped raining," Barbara said.

Zaire had secretly hoped that it would continue to rain, forcing everyone to stay inside the house. She walked over to the French doors leading to the patio and stared out. The outdoor kitchen, complete with grill, pizza oven, ice maker and refrigerator, was designed to match the Mediterranean style of the rest of the house.

Her father was getting the grill ready.

Before the attack, Zaire had spent a lot of time on the

patio. She would sometimes get up early and work out or go swimming. Afterward, she and her mother would have breakfast together near the Olympic-size pool.

She glanced over her shoulder. Her mother was busy preparing the fish and chicken for cooking on the grill.

Zaire gave the patio one last glance and then joined Barbara in the kitchen. She retrieved the bowl containing the ground beef from the fridge and placed it on the counter. "I'll make the burgers."

"Thanks, sweetie," her mother responded.

"I told Tyrese he may want to bring some balling clothes," Zaire said, trying to make conversation as she manipulated the meat into patties. "I'm sure Ari and Blaze are going to try and engage him into a game."

Barbara chuckled. "You're right about that."

Zaire stared longingly at the French doors leading to the patio.

"Would you like to try going outside?" her mother asked.

She nodded. "I think I'm ready."

The attack had happened almost three months ago. Her therapist had informed Zaire that she was doing well, and if she continued progressing, the sessions would no longer be necessary.

Zaire walked to the door and opened it.

Her father was outside. When Malcolm spied her standing in the doorway, he walked over and held out his hand. "You can do it, sweetie."

Zaire could feel her chest tightening, but she focused

her attention on the beauty of her surroundings. "There is nothing to fear," she whispered.

Tyrese walked up and stood beside her father. His smile warmed her all over. "Come to me."

She focused on his gorgeous eyes and sexy grin. Zaire stepped outside, pausing for a moment before taking another step.

Tyrese held out his hand to her.

Zaire took another tentative step. Her chest felt tight, and she felt as though it was getting hard to breathe. She took several calming breaths. "Nothing to fear," she whispered. "I can do this, and nothing is going to happen."

"You're doing great," Tyrese told her. "I'm so proud of you."

Zaire practically fell into his arms. "I did it...."

He kissed her mouth. "Yes, you did, baby."

She glanced over at her father and said, "Thanks for being here, Daddy."

Tyrese escorted her over to a nearby table. "Would you like something to drink?" he asked.

"Could you get me some lemonade, please?"

"Look who has decided to come outside," Blaze murmured. "Hey, sis." He and Livi had just arrived. They had decided to walk along the side of the house to the patio instead of going inside.

Livi sat down at the table with Zaire. "Let me know when you're ready to get back to Zumba. I've missed my workout partner."

"I will," Zaire promised.

She felt blissfully happy and fully alive for the first time in a long time. Her eyes strayed to where Tyrese stood chatting with her father and Blaze. He gave her a huge smile.

Zaire gloried in their shared moment.

Tyrese had not had this much fun in a long time. He played a couple of rounds of basketball with Zaire's brothers until it started to rain, sending everyone inside the house.

"The day that I walk out to the patio is the day that it decides to storm," Zaire complained.

Tyrese embraced her. "I don't care where we are as long as we're together," he whispered.

Drayden found two decks of cards, prompting a discussion of who was good when it came to playing Spades.

"You don't want none of this over here," Blaze said with a grin. "Livi and I don't lose."

"That's because you haven't played me and Natasha," Ari countered.

Sage broke into a short laugh. "My honey and I will put the rest of you to shame. Won't we, baby?"

Ryan grinned and nodded.

Tyrese and Zaire decided to just watch rather than play.

They sat in a corner of the family room talking.

"I've been thinking about asking Franklin to teach me some self-defense techniques," Zaire told Tyrese. "I just have to catch him because he travels frequently."

"I can teach you."

She looked at Tyrese. "What are you? A black belt or something?"

"Actually, I am," Tyrese admitted.

"Now, why am I just hearing about this?" Zaire asked. "I had no idea."

"I was going to suggest that I teach you, but I was waiting for the right time."

"I want to get started as soon as possible," she told him. "Tyrese, I never want to feel that helpless again during my lifetime. I'm actually thinking about taking a tae-kwon-do class."

"I think you should if that's what you want to do, sweetheart."

"Can we get started on Monday?" she asked.

Tyrese nodded. "Sure."

An expression of satisfaction showed in her eyes. Zaire leaned against him and sighed. "I knew you were the man for me the moment I saw you."

He chuckled. "I had the same thought when I saw you."

"Really?"

His features became more animated. "Yes. I said to myself, 'I am definitely the man for this woman.'"

Zaire broke into laughter.

"The first thing we are going to do is work on core-strengthening exercises," Tyrese said.

Zaire glanced over at him and smiled. "Let's do this."

His gaze traveled down from her neck to the sports

bra she was wearing and downward. She looked sexy in her workout clothes.

Tyrese forced himself to focus on the reason he was there.

"While we are training, I want you to keep self-defense in mind," he said after the warm-up exercises. "Everything I teach you should be filled with intensity and purpose. Take nothing for granted because it could save your life."

Zaire listened attentively. She was determined to take back control of her life.

"An elbow strike is really effective if someone is against your back or preparing to grab you around your waist," Tyrese explained. "Make a fist with the same hand…"

She did as he directed.

"Use your entire torso to throw your elbow."

They practiced the move several times.

"Another part of your body that can be used as a weapon is your feet," Tyrese told her. "Kicking is the best deployment of the foot. Kicking to the front or sides of the knees will disable your attacker."

"I would aim straight for the groin," Zaire said. "That's what I tried to do to that jerk."

"Kicking blindly gave him the opportunity to grab your leg."

She nodded.

"Women need to use the element of surprise as part of your overall defense. Your attacker can't know what you're about to do."

"Great job today," Tyrese told her at the end of their workout.

"You're a good teacher."

"Thank you, ma'am." He broke into a grin. "Honey, you have displayed such courage and determination throughout all you've been through. I want you to know that I'm so proud of you."

"I feel empowered," she replied. "I am not going to keep hiding from the world. I am going to beat this thing."

The Christmas holidays were approaching and Zaire did not want to miss out on the thrill of shopping for presents for her family and friends. She wanted her life back.

Chapter 14

Zaire glanced anxiously over at her therapist and then back at the car parked in the driveway. "I'm ready."

"Open the door."

She placed trembling fingers around the handle. "I can do this," she whispered over and over. "There's nothing to be afraid of…."

Zaire released a soft sigh. "Doors are open and I'm okay."

"Very good. Are you ready to get inside of the car? Just take one step."

She nodded.

Zaire felt empowered at having gotten this far. She had been riding for short distances with her mother and Tyrese. Today, she was going to drive.

She felt the tightness dissipate and smiled. Zaire

couldn't wait to get back home and call Tyrese to give him a recap. She was a lucky woman to have found a man who was so supportive. He had been by her side every step of the way as promised. Even when it went against his seemingly better judgment, Tyrese never abandoned her.

Zaire appreciated such loyalty and devotion. It was those qualities that true love was made of. Okay, she was a romantic. Nothing was wrong with that, she reasoned.

Once she started driving, Zaire calmed down and enjoyed the scenery. Her therapist did not have her drive too far as this was just the first day.

"You can turn around here and head back to the house."

Back at home, Zaire felt giddy.

She felt as if she had earned a little release of freedom. Words could not express what she was feeling right now. It was exhilarating to be able to enjoy the outdoors once again and to drive just a short distance. It was a tiny accomplishment, but Zaire felt as if she had moved a mountain. It gave her the motivation to continue pushing forward. *This is my Christmas present to myself,* she thought.

A smile tugged at her lips. She also owed some of the credit to Tyrese. Zaire had meant it when she'd told him that he had saved her life.

If only she could get him to fully release his heart to her safekeeping.

Tyrese did not have to tell her that he was afraid of

being hurt by love. She could see it in his eyes. The woman from his past had wounded him deeply, although he would never admit it.

Zaire dabbed her face with her towel. "That was some workout. I feel good, though."

"Why don't you go shower and get changed," Tyrese suggested. "I'll shower down here."

"Where are we going?" she asked, wearing a puzzled expression on her face.

"I want to take you to dinner. We don't have to go far, but let's get out of the house for a while. If you feel up to it, we can take a stroll on the beach afterward."

She nodded. "It's fine. I'll be ready in a few minutes."

Zaire hummed softly as she rushed up the stairs. She was looking forward to going out with Tyrese. It did not matter to her where they were going. Zaire was just happy to spend time with him. She enjoyed his company immensely.

An hour later, they were seated in a booth at a local Italian restaurant.

"You have quite the sense of humor," Zaire commented as she scanned her menu. She took a sip of her ice water. "I really like this side of you."

He laughed. "I take it that you thought I was pretty boring."

"Not really," she replied. "Well...I felt like you needed something more than work in your life."

"I remember you telling me that."

She met his gaze. "I hope that I didn't make you feel bad."

"You didn't." Tyrese reached across the table to hold her hand. "I have to confess that you were right. All of my focus was on building the company until I met you."

"Any regrets?" Zaire asked.

He shook his head. "Not at all."

Tyrese picked up his menu and looked it over. "I think I'm having the chicken marsala," he said. "Do you know what you want?"

"I'm in the mood for spaghetti."

They gave the waiter their orders when he returned to the table.

"I have to admit that I haven't had as much fun as I've had with you and your family," Tyrese confessed after the waiter had walked away. "I appreciate the way they have gone out of the way to make me comfortable."

"My family really likes you," Zaire stated with a tender smile.

"I like them, too."

The waiter returned with their food on a tray.

Tyrese blessed the food.

Zaire sampled her spaghetti. "This is delicious."

"This is really good," he responded. "Have you tried this entrée before?"

She nodded. "I think I've probably tried every selection on the menu. I love this place. It's one of my favorite restaurants." Zaire's eyes traveled the dining area. "It feels good being out like this among people. I've missed this."

After signaling for the check a short time later, Tyrese inquired, "Are you feeling up to a moonlit stroll on the beach?"

She awarded him a smile. "Definitely."

They left the restaurant and parked near a set of stairs leading down to the beach. Tyrese held on to Zaire tightly.

She removed her shoes, and he did the same.

They strolled along the edge of the beach hand in hand.

Zaire closed her eyes, savoring the feel of the night air on her face.

Tyrese pulled her into his arms. "I can't believe that I found someone as wonderful as you, Zaire." He wrapped his arm around her waist.

She felt the heat of desire wash over her like waves.

Turning her face upward, Tyrese kissed her lips. "You make me feel things I haven't felt in a very long time."

"I feel the same way about you, Tyrese. No man has ever made me feel the way you have."

He kissed her again.

Zaire buried her face against his chest, enjoying the feel of Tyrese's muscled arms around her.

"Why are you so quiet all of a sudden?" he asked after a moment.

"I was just thinking about how lucky I am to have a man like you in my life. You made something that was horrible—you made it bearable. You wouldn't just let me hide away from the world."

"I hope you know that I won't ever let anything happen to you, Zaire. I would rather die first than let someone ever hurt you again."

She looked up at him and smiled. "You are my hero."

Chapter 15

The therapy sessions and the self-defense training had done wonders for Zaire. She was not only able to leave the house during the holidays, but she had resumed swimming in the pool and she could drive short distances as long as someone was in the car with her.

However, Zaire wasn't quite ready to return to M.G. She no longer had nightmares about the attack, but she was not yet ready to be near the parking structure.

Tyrese supported her decision to continue working from home for now. She worked from home and continued to be very productive.

"I have a webinar starting shortly," she told him when he called to check on her. "Can I call you back afterward?"

"Sure."

"Great. I'll talk to you then."

Zaire disconnected the call and then dialed up her assistant. "Max, are you all set?"

She was especially excited about this special event to launch a new fashion magazine for plus-size women.

"I sure am," he responded.

The webinar lasted for an hour and fifteen minutes.

Zaire touched base with Max afterward. "Email the contract to them and let me know when you receive the signed copies back."

Her next phone call was to Tyrese.

"How did it go?" he asked.

"Max is sending the contracts over as we speak," she replied. "They loved the proposal."

"I'm not surprised."

"You're sweet," Zaire told Tyrese. "I love that you're so supportive."

"Same here," he responded.

Tyrese changed the tone of the conversation by saying, "I called you because I wanted to let you know that I have to go out of town for a few days. Pilar and I are looking for offices in New York."

"How long will you be gone?" Zaire wanted to know.

"I won't be back until Saturday morning."

"Four days," she murmured. "I guess I can manage without you for four days."

Tyrese chuckled. "Of that, I have no doubt. I wish you could go with me."

"I'm not ready for that," Zaire confessed. "I am going to miss you like crazy, though."

Her mother was outside tending to her rose garden when Zaire finished her conversation with Tyrese.

"The flowers are gorgeous," she told Barbara.

"They turned out nicely, didn't they? I hope your aunt is taking good care of my roses back home in Aspen."

"Aunt Bess loves flowers as much as you do," Zaire stated. "I'm sure she's treating them as if they were her own."

Barbara chuckled. "I hear she's had the house completely repainted and is adding a bigger kitchen."

Malcolm and Barbara had gifted their former home to her sister after they'd relocated to California. Zaire knew that her aunt had been deeply touched by the gesture. She had never been able to afford her own home, but now she had one that was mortgage-free and she lived in it with pride.

"Speaking of homes," Zaire began. "Mama, I think it's time I went back to my apartment."

"Are you sure?"

Zaire nodded. "I need to resume my life. I can have Tyrese or Max drive me around if I need to go anywhere."

"You don't have to rush this," Barbara said. "You can stay here for as long as you like."

"I'm not rushing into this decision," Zaire replied. "It's been four and a half months since the attack. If I keep hiding out, my attacker wins."

"Why don't you have Franklin stay with you until

you get used to being there alone?" her mother suggested.

"Tyrese actually offered to stay with me." Zaire saw the expression on her mother's face and added, "He's going to sleep in the guest bedroom."

"Uh-huh…" Barbara uttered.

"Mama, don't you trust me?"

She smiled. "Trust has nothing to do with it. I know what happens between two people who are in love."

"It's because I love him that I'm not going to rush into bed with Tyrese," Zaire told her mother. "I'm not looking for a boy toy. I want a husband."

Zaire moved back into her apartment a week after Tyrese returned from New York.

"Are you okay?" Tyrese asked.

She walked around, going from room to room, checking to see if anything was out of place.

"I had my housekeeper come over to dust and clean," he said.

She glanced over her shoulder at him and smiled. "Thanks. I don't know what I'd do without you."

"Hopefully, you will never have to find out."

Zaire sank down on her sofa. "I wasn't sure how I'd feel about coming back here, but it feels right. I feel like I'm home."

Tyrese grabbed her hand and pulled her to her feet. "C'mon—I have a surprise for you."

"What is it?" she asked.

He led her into the dining room.

Vibrant flames in red and gold flickered from the silver-colored candles, casting a soft glow on the succulent display of baked chicken, roasted potatoes, yeast rolls and steaming broccoli.

Zaire eyed the beautifully decorated table. "Everything looks delicious."

Tyrese pulled out a chair for her.

"Thank you," Zaire murmured as she sat down. Tyrese walked around the table and eased into a chair facing her. "Did you cook all this?"

Tyrese nodded.

"You did a wonderful job. Thank you for everything—especially for moving into my tiny little apartment. Hopefully, I'll be able to stay here by myself soon."

He smiled. "You will. Zaire, you are a lot stronger than you realize."

After dinner, Tyrese sent her to relax while he cleaned the kitchen. This was a first for Zaire. None of the men she had dated in the past ever entered the kitchen unless it was to find something to eat or drink.

He joined her on the sofa. Zaire curled up beside him.

"This has been a wonderful homecoming."

Tyrese kissed her on the cheek. "I'm glad. I really wanted to impress you with my culinary skills."

"I'm definitely impressed, Tyrese. No one has ever treated me the way you do. It's kind of foreign. Do you know what I mean?"

"I do," he responded. "Zaire, I feel the same way about you. I've never met a woman like you."

Moving closer, she laid her head on his chest and closed her eyes.

An hour later, Tyrese gently woke Zaire up. "Why don't you go to bed, sweetheart? You're exhausted."

She flushed in embarrassment. "Did I fall asleep? Tyrese, I'm so sorry."

"It's fine," he assured her.

Zaire stifled a yawn.

"C'mon—let's get you to bed."

Tyrese escorted her to the master bedroom.

"I feel awful," Zaire said. "I didn't realize I was so tired." She ached so much for his touch. She wanted to feel his arms wrapped around her like a warm blanket. Her emotions melted her resolve. "I don't want you to leave, Tyrese. I want you to stay with me."

"Are you sure about this?" he wanted to know. His steady gaze bored into her in silent expectation.

"We're both adults," she stated. "I'm sure we can share a bed without it leading to sex."

Tyrese wasn't so sure, but he did not respond.

He sat on the edge of her king-size bed while Zaire changed in the bathroom.

When she walked out in a pair of silk pajama pants and a camisole, his breath caught in his throat.

She pulled down the comforter and climbed into bed.

Tyrese stood there watching her.

"Are you coming to bed?" she asked him.

"I need to change," Tyrese responded. "I'll be right back."

Their gazes locked for a moment.

Both of them could see the attraction mirrored in the other's eyes.

The smoldering flame Zaire saw in Tyrese's eyes held her spellbound.

He broke the gaze and turned on his heel, walking toward the door.

In the guest bedroom, Tyrese sank down on the edge of the bed. He had no idea how he was going to sleep beside Zaire and not make love to her. It was a constant struggle being in the same room with her.

Even the prolonged anticipation of lying in bed kissing her had become unbearable. His body craved the feel of her skin against his own.

Tyrese rose to his feet and walked briskly across the carpeted floor to the bathroom. He was going to need a cold shower.

Tyrese prayed that Zaire had fallen asleep by the time he returned to her room.

She was wide-awake.

He climbed into bed beside her.

She snuggled up to him. "You smell good."

"Zaire, I have a confession to make," he said.

"What is it?"

"This is torture."

Zaire sat up, propping herself against a couple of pillows. "I'm sorry."

Tyrese sat up, as well. "It's not your fault that you're so incredibly sexy. I blame your parents."

She laughed.

"Maybe this isn't such a good idea."

"Tyrese, you don't have to sleep in here with me. I'll be okay."

He pulled her into his arms. "I'll stay with you until you fall asleep."

Zaire released a sigh of relief. "Thank you."

Tyrese held her close to him as he savored every moment.

It did not take long for Zaire to fall asleep. He watched her for a while before easing out of bed.

A large part of Tyrese did not want to leave, but it was for the best. If he stayed, he would not get any sleep at all, and he had a long day tomorrow.

The next morning, Tyrese had breakfast ready by the time Zaire walked out of her bedroom.

"You're spoiling me."

He awarded her a smile. "I intend to do a lot of that," Tyrese told her. "I hope you don't mind."

Zaire sat down at the breakfast table. "Not as long as you allow me to spoil you in return."

They dined on scrambled eggs, bacon and toast.

"I see I'm going to have to show off my skills in the kitchen," Zaire said. "I'm making dinner for us tonight."

Tyrese liked seeing the vibrancy return in her. She'd slept through the night without having a nightmare.

"What are your plans for the day?" he asked. "Besides cooking dinner tonight."

"I'm going to try and get the Daniels Auto retreat finalized. It's not that far away, and I want everything to be perfect."

"Bill's very pleased with everything you have done. I think you've won a fan for life. He is already talking about having you plan a surprise birthday party for his wife."

"He's been really easy to work with." Zaire took a sip of her cranberry juice. "So has Harold. I've really enjoyed working with them both."

They finished up breakfast.

"I'll take care of the kitchen," Zaire told him as she rose to her feet. "You need to get ready for work."

Tyrese stood up and pulled her into his arms. "I really hate leaving you today."

She kissed him. "I'm going to be fine. Sage is coming by to visit with me this afternoon."

"I'll check on you throughout the day."

Zaire pushed him out of the kitchen. "Go get dressed."

He kissed her once more. "I love you."

She smiled. "I know."

An hour later, Zaire was seated at her desk going over the timeline for the upcoming Daniels Auto retreat with Max on speakerphone.

"I will be speaking with Bill later this afternoon," she told her assistant. "After I talk to him, I'll give you a call back on the agenda for the welcome reception."

She hung up the phone just as the doorbell sounded.

Zaire knew it was Sage because of the text she'd received just seconds before. Still, she checked the video monitor feed from the security camera that was installed in the hallway—it was one of the reasons she'd chosen to live in this building.

She opened the door and stepped aside to let her sister enter the apartment.

They embraced before settling down in the living room.

"How does it feel to be back here?" Sage asked.

"It's great," Zaire responded. "I'm not sure how I will handle being here alone at night, though."

"Mama said that Tyrese has moved in with you."

"He's more like a roommate, Sage. We sleep in separate rooms."

Her sister was surprised. "Really? You two haven't…"

Zaire shook her head. "I've had to deal with a lot, and I don't want to jump into a physical relationship with Tyrese until I know that I have me back on track."

Sage smiled in approval. "I think that's a wise decision."

"Don't get me wrong," Zaire said. "I love him so much and I want to take our relationship to the next level."

"You have time, sis. You don't have to rush it."

"It's not easy, though. Tyrese is so handsome and he's sexy…." Zaire shook her head. "He treats me like a queen."

"I think I like him," Sage responded. "As long as he's good to you—I don't have a problem with him."

"I don't think you have anything to worry about. Tyrese is a good man, and I know that he loves me."

Zaire reached over and placed her hand on Sage's belly. "Hello, little baby."

"I'm so ready to meet him or her," Sage told Zaire.

"I don't know why you and Ryan wanted to wait to find out the sex. I would want to know as soon as possible."

"We just want to be surprised."

Zaire ordered lunch for her and Sage.

While they waited for the food to arrive, she showed her sister some of the plans she had arranged for Harold DePaul. "He says that he's pleased with what I've done so far."

"I haven't seen him much, but Meredith says that he's been doing a lot of traveling. She's been trying to get him to come to one of the cookouts."

"I invited him, too," Zaire said. "It would be really nice if the Alexander and DePaul family members could come together as one. Just think of what we could accomplish in terms of helping those less fortunate."

Sage agreed, "We could have been a great team in the hotel industry, as well."

Chapter 16

Zaire finished her conversation with Bill Daniels and then hung up the telephone. She picked up another folder and opened it.

She called her assistant afterward. "Hey, Max. I need you to do something for me. We need the perfect location for the Honore' Designs party during Fashion Week."

"Sounds like fun."

Zaire grinned. "I know, huh?"

"I'll get right on it."

"Thanks so much, Max. I really appreciate you."

"And I really miss you, Zaire. I hope you'll come back to the office soon."

"I'm working on it."

She opened up a packet that had been sent to the

office for her. Tyrese had brought it home with him a couple of days ago, but Zaire had forgotten about it until now. She tore open the envelope.

A smile spread across her face as she read the information contained on the brochure. Zaire picked up her cell phone and dialed.

"Harold, it's Zaire," she said. "I have the perfect place for your retreat."

"Really? Where?"

"The French Riviera," she announced. "You can rent Villa Valmer for the week or just the weekend. There is the main house, a guesthouse and staff quarters for a total of twelve bedrooms, eleven bathrooms. It's four acres on the waterfront, which is fenced in for privacy."

"I like what I'm hearing so far," Harold responded.

"The home was built in 1903 by Henri Paul Nénot. I think it's the perfect location for what you have in mind."

Harold said, "I'd like to see the place in person, if you can arrange it. In fact, it would be nice to have you and Tyrese join me."

"Are you serious?" Zaire asked. "You want us to go to the French Riviera with you for a few days?" She was surprised by his invitation.

"Yes. Before we commit to hosting the retreat there— I think we should see it first."

"I agree," she responded. "I'll talk to Tyrese and get back to you. In the meantime, I'll email you some photographs of the villa."

"I know you've been through a lot, Zaire. Maybe getting away for a few days will help."

"Thanks, Harold. I appreciate your thoughtfulness."

"Has there been any news on your attacker?"

"No," she said. "There are no real clear images on the security cameras."

"Meredith told me that you wanted to sell your car."

"I do. I want something a little more low-key," Zaire replied. "Are you interested in buying it?"

"Actually, I have a friend who wants one. I'm sure he'd want to get it. If you like, I can give him your email address."

"That's fine," she said. "I'll email you photos of the car."

There was a momentary silence on the phone.

"How is William?" Zaire inquired, referring to Harold's older brother, who had been ill.

"He's not doing well," Harold said quietly. "I don't think he's going to be with us much longer."

"I'm sorry, Harold."

"I wasted a lot of time being angry with him for not siding with me. I'll never get that time back."

"But you still have today," Zaire told him. "Make the best of every moment that you have with him."

"William's made me realize just how important family should be," he said. "I'm tired of losing people I love."

Zaire heard the sadness in his voice. "Harold, if you need us, please don't be afraid to let someone know. We are a part of your family despite the color of our skin."

"After all I've done to your family…you still want to have a relationship with me."

"All families have some form of drama," she said with a chuckle.

"Thank you, Zaire. For everything."

"We're still waiting to see you at the family cookouts on the weekend."

He gave a short laugh. "I'll get there. I give you my word."

Zaire hung up. She picked up the brochure and the photographs of the villa. "This is the perfect place for Harold's retreat."

She was not sure if she was ready to get on a plane and travel all the way to France, although Zaire agreed that a nice little getaway from everything might be just what she needed.

When Tyrese walked into the apartment, he found Zaire sound asleep on the sofa. He smiled while watching her sleep. He planted a soft kiss on her forehead.

She stirred but did not wake up.

He kissed her again, moving his mouth over hers, devouring its softness.

Zaire let out a soft moan.

"Wake up, sleepyhead."

Zaire opened her eyes, stretched and yawned. "When did you get home?"

"Not too long ago."

She sat up and swung her legs off the sofa. "What time is it?"

"Seven-thirty," Tyrese replied.

"I had no idea I'd been asleep this long," she murmured. "I lay down to take a thirty-minute power nap. I slept for almost three hours."

"You must have been tired," he told her.

Zaire planted a kiss on his lips. "I'm glad that you're home. Are you hungry?"

Tyrese shook his head. "I grabbed a sandwich earlier."

She picked up the brochure lying on the table and said, "This is where Harold should host his retreat."

Tyrese surveyed the brochure. "It's nice," he murmured. "What does he think?"

"He wants to see it in person." Zaire stifled another yawn. "In fact, he wants you and me to go to France with him."

"Really?"

His cell phone rang.

Zaire looked at him. "Do you need to get that?"

Tyrese shook his head. His stomach was filled with apprehension. He hoped that Zaire would not become suspicious. He did not want her getting upset over nothing.

Gathering her into his arms, he held her snugly.

She yawned again, prompting him to say, "You're really tired. Why don't you make it an early night?"

"No," she protested. "I haven't seen you all day. I just want to spend some time with you. Tell me about your day."

Tyrese laughed. "I don't want to bore you with the details."

"I'm really interested," she said. "Did you snag Delta Airlines?"

"As a matter of fact, I did."

She hugged him. "Congratulations, Ty."

"Don't call me that," he stated firmly.

His response seemed to catch Zaire off guard. "Okaay... you want to tell me what *that* was about?"

"I'm sorry. I didn't mean to snap at you like that."

"So why did you react that way?" she asked him.

Tyrese really did not want to have this discussion. "Honey, it's nothing. I'm just tired."

Zaire looked as if she didn't believe him, but she did not press him further. Instead, she rose to her feet. "I think I'm going to take a shower and slip into a pair of pajamas."

Tyrese wasn't sure whether or not she was upset with him. He decided to just let the entire matter drop completely.

He was still in the living room when Zaire walked out of her bedroom. She sat down beside him with her iPad.

Tyrese scanned her face. "You know that I love you, don't you?"

Zaire nodded but did not look up at him.

She's angry.

He tried handing her the television remote.

"I don't need it," Zaire told him.

"Please don't be angry," he said. "I shouldn't have

been short with you, Zaire. All I can do is apologize to you."

Tyrese rose to his feet and crossed the room in quick strides. He peeked out of the window before turning his attention back to Zaire. "It's a beautiful night. The sky is clear."

Zaire stood up and joined him at the window. "It is a nice night."

He turned and looked down at her. "The scenery in here is much more beautiful, in my opinion."

She smiled. "You really know how to woo a girl."

Tyrese embraced her, holding her tight against his body. He loved the way she fitted in his arms. It was as if Zaire had been made just for him.

"I don't ever want to lose you," he whispered into her hair.

"You never have to worry about that," Zaire responded. "We are a team for life."

"Maybe I should get that in writing."

His infectious grin set the tone. She laughed. "Honey, I love you so much. You are *that guy*."

"And you are *that girl*."

"Prove it," Zaire whispered.

His lips descended slowly to meet hers.

"Livi, can you do me a favor?" Zaire called her sister-in-law early the next morning. "I hope I didn't wake you or Blaze."

"You're fine," Livi assured her. "Blaze isn't here,

but we've been up for hours. What's going on? What do you need?"

"I need a gown for a charity event that's happening tonight. I want to surprise Tyrese. He asked me to go with him, but I told him that I wasn't up to being around so many people."

"I actually have the perfect dress for you," she told Zaire. "I'll drop it off in a couple of hours."

She released an audible sigh of relief. "Great. Thanks so much. I didn't know what I was going to do about a gown. I didn't want to wear one I already own because I've been photographed in them."

"You don't have to worry," Livi said. "You are going to be the best-looking woman at the charity ball."

"Now I just need to order a car. I'm a little nervous about it, but I have to do this. Tyrese is getting an award, and I need to be there to support him."

"Zaire, we're going to the event tonight," Livi announced. "Do you want to ride with us?"

"That would be great," she said. "I would be much calmer riding with you and Blaze."

"I'm going to put together a complete outfit for you from top to bottom. You just sit back and relax."

"My hairstylist is coming by in an hour and she's bringing someone to do my mani-pedi."

Zaire wanted the evening to be perfect. It would be her first public appearance since the attack. Tyrese was going to be surprised to see her there. He had originally planned to bow out, but she had convinced him to attend

since his company was receiving an award. Pilar knew
that she was attending and had secured her invitation.

Her sister-in-law arrived shortly after eleven o'clock.

"Livi, this dress is gorgeous," Zaire exclaimed. "It's
perfect."

"I'm glad you like it. It will look stunning on you."

She hugged Livi. "Thanks so much for your help."
Zaire opened the shoe box. "Wow…I love them."

Livi picked up her purse and car keys. "I need to get
to my office, but call me if you need anything else."

"Thanks again," she said. "Oh, put everything on
my credit card. You should have it on file."

"This is a gift from me," Livi told her. "We'll pick
you up at seven."

"I'll be ready."

Zaire turned on the radio.

She loved music, and it had been a while since she
had listened to music in any form. Zaire danced around
the living room as she sang the words to a Mary J.
Blige song.

She no longer felt like a victim. She was free and
that freedom was worth celebrating, in Zaire's opinion.

"I don't feel right being here without Zaire," Tyrese
told Pilar. He had been there for less than twenty minutes, but he was already preparing to leave. "She's at
home alone, and I'm not sure she's ready for that."

"It's only for a few hours. She'll be fine."

"Pilar, she's been through a lot and she's doing well,
but I don't want anything to set her back." He pulled at

his collar. "Do me a favor and accept the award for me. I'm going home to Zaire."

"I don't think you have anything to worry about." Pilar looked past Tyrese and smiled.

He followed her gaze.

Tyrese's mouth dropped open at the sight of Zaire. She looked exquisite in the silver strapless gown that hugged her curves as if it were made just for her. The pleat and rhinestone beading added a sophisticated touch to the dress.

Zaire smiled and waved to a couple of people as she made her way over to Tyrese and Pilar.

The two women embraced.

"I'm glad you showed up when you did," Pilar stated. "I don't think I was going to be able to keep him here a minute longer. Girl, he was about to get up out of here. He was worried about you."

She met his smile. "That's so sweet."

"Well, I see a couple of people I need to talk to," Pilar announced. "I'll see you both in a few minutes."

"You look beautiful," Tyrese told her when they were alone. "Why didn't you tell me that you wanted to come?"

She grinned. "It wouldn't have been a surprise if I'd done that. There was no way that I'd miss this night. I have to be here for you the same way you have been there for me." The warmth of her smile was echoed in her voice.

"I'm glad that you're here," Tyrese said. "I was just about to leave because I wanted to be home with you."

"I'm here now, so let's enjoy the evening."

He met her gaze. "Are you sure you wouldn't prefer to just get out of here? We could go home where it's just the two of us."

"That does sound tempting," Zaire murmured softly.

"We can leave right now."

She gave him a generous smile. "No, we can't. I have on this gorgeous gown, and I look stunning. But more than that, you are going to be honored tonight for all you've done for this charity. Tyrese, we are not going to miss this."

"I just want you all to myself."

"We have tonight," she whispered. "For the first time in a long time, I feel like me. I still have a ways to go, but I've come a long way. Tonight, when we get home, we are going to celebrate."

"Zaire…"

She tingled as he said her name. "C'mon—let's make our rounds and then we'll get in line for the buffet."

A shiver of wanting ran through Tyrese. "We are not staying one moment longer than we have to be here," he told Zaire.

She nodded in agreement.

They had been waiting for this moment for what seemed like a lifetime.

Tyrese's hand brushed against hers, which Zaire found soft and caressing, and it sent shivers of delight through her.

Zaire was happy, her mood buoyant.

He took her around the room, introducing her to

many of the attendees she had not met yet. Afterward, they walked over to their table and sat down.

Her brother and Livi were seated at the next table. Blaze walked over to her and asked, "Save a dance for me, okay?"

"Definitely," she responded.

Tyrese excused himself. "I'm going to get something for us to drink."

"You know I wasn't sure about Tyrese and you at first, but the more I see you two together...I think he's good for you."

Zaire glanced over her shoulder, and then back at her brother. "He's wonderful, Blaze. I am so in love with Tyrese."

"I'm glad he makes you happy."

"He does," Zaire confirmed. "He really does."

Tyrese returned with their drinks.

They both tried to focus on the event going on around them but could not.

Zaire glanced over at Tyrese and gave him a knowing smile. She was counting down to the time when they could slip out of the ballroom. She hungered for him. Zaire wanted to feel his skin next to hers.

She was so ready to take their relationship to the next level. It was not just about the sex for her. Her whole being seem to be filled with longing to be united with the only man she had ever loved deep down to her soul.

"I can't tell you how glad I am to be home," Tyrese said as soon as they walked into the apartment.

Zaire laid her purse on a nearby sofa table. "I am, too." She loved that he considered her apartment his home, as well. Tyrese owned a five-bedroom home in Hollywood Hills, but he had chosen to stay here with her until she felt completely safe. He had been willing to sacrifice his comfort for her—one more reason why she loved him.

She pointed toward the bedroom. "I'm going to get comfortable. Why don't you make some tea?"

He nodded.

She navigated to her bedroom.

Despite her outward calm, Zaire was nervous, but she hid her feelings from Tyrese. She didn't want him to consider postponing what was about to happen.

She opened her lingerie drawer and pulled out the gown she had been waiting to wear for him.

Zaire walked into the living room a few minutes later, wearing a turquoise silk gown and matching robe. The gown featured a thigh-high slit, showing off her left leg as she glided across the hardwood floor in a pair of high-heeled turquoise-and-silver sandals.

Tyrese was speechless as he looked her over seductively.

She sat down beside him.

He pointed to the cup on the coffee table. "You should drink your tea before it gets cold."

Tyrese looked at her as if he were photographing her with his eyes. His gaze dropped from her eyes to her shoulders and continued downward.

Zaire took a sip of the hot drink. "It's good."

His gaze rose back up to her face and searched her eyes. Something intense flared through his entrancement.

Tyrese stood up and removed his tuxedo jacket.

Zaire admired his firm, muscled arms beneath his crisp white shirt. His broad shoulders were heaving as he breathed.

Tyrese held out his hands to her.

She allowed him to pull her to her feet.

He wrapped his arms around her midriff. "You are so beautiful," he murmured. "I love everything about you without qualification. I want you to know that. I never realized just how lonely my life had become until I met you, Zaire."

"I'm a very lucky woman."

He grinned. "Yes, you are."

"You are such a humble man," she murmured with a short laugh.

His arms encircled Zaire, one hand at the small of her back. "Seriously, I am the one who's lucky. I never thought I would meet a woman like you, much less have her love me. You are much more than I ever dared hope for."

She locked herself into his embrace. "I will always love you, Tyrese."

His mouth covered hers hungrily, sending spirals of ecstasy through her.

Tyrese picked her up and carried her into the bedroom, placing her gently on the bed.

Zaire breathed lightly between parted lips as she

watched him walk in confident strides to the door, closing it. She felt as if she had been transported on a soft and wispy cloud. Tonight was perfect.

Chapter 17

The next morning, Tyrese was clearly surprised when Zaire strolled into the kitchen wearing a chic pantsuit and carrying her red tote. Her smile broadened at the sight of him.

"Going somewhere?" he asked her.

She joined him at the breakfast table. "I think it's time I go back to the office. I've been away too long."

He smiled.

"Are you okay with this?" Zaire questioned. "Our driving to the office together?" She had a new car, but the thought of parking in the garage at work ignited anxiety in her. She needed more time to get over her fear.

"I don't care if the others know that we're together," Tyrese responded. "I'm sure they already suspect something."

"As happy as I am right now, I'm sure the staff will pick up on it as soon as I step off the elevator." Zaire looked at him. "After last night, I feel truly connected to you."

He reached over and gave her hand a light squeeze.

"What do you want for breakfast?" she asked, looking at the wall clock. "We need to get out of here soon."

Tyrese pointed to his cup of coffee. "I'm fine."

Zaire grabbed an apple and some yogurt from the fridge. "I'm ready when you are."

They left the apartment and headed down to the car.

She was determined to prove to herself that her anxiety would not hold her prisoner any longer. Zaire stole a peek over at Tyrese. She had so many reasons to live her life to the fullest.

Her determination faltered as they neared San Vincente Boulevard. Zaire began to shake as fearful images built in her mind.

As if sensing her discomfort, Tyrese reached over, taking her hand in his. "Honey, you okay?"

"I'm fine."

Zaire leaned back and closed her eyes, using the techniques she had learned to calm herself. A flicker of apprehension coursed through her when the parking deck came into view.

Tyrese gave her hand a gentle massage. "It's okay, baby. I've made lots of changes. There are cameras everywhere. You're safe. I'm here and I will die before I let anyone ever hurt you again."

She took several calming breaths. "I'll be fine."

He parked the car, got out and walked around to open the door for her.

Zaire's chest felt tight, but she concentrated on pleasant thoughts. As they walked into the building, her tension eased away gradually. Tyrese remained close by her side.

He made sure that she was settled in her office before he walked down the hall to his own.

Max blew into her office, saying, "I'm so glad that you're back."

She laughed. "Good morning."

"I'm going to make you some herbal tea, and then we are going to get down to business. The Daniels Auto retreat is just weeks away."

Zaire set up her laptop and turned it on. "We need to finalize the Honore' event, as well."

"I'll be right back."

She glanced around her office, realizing for the first time just how much she had missed being in the office. It was good to be back.

Tyrese glanced down at the caller ID and frowned. Although the caller's identity was blocked, he knew exactly who was calling.

As always, he let the call go to voice mail.

Zaire knocked on his door. "Hey, I thought we were having lunch together? Are you still able to make it?"

Tyrese tugged at the collar of his shirt. "Honey, I'm sorry. Time slipped by me." He pushed away from his desk and stood up. "I'm ready."

They walked across the street to the restaurant on the corner.

"You seem a bit preoccupied, Tyrese," Zaire observed. "Is everything okay?"

He picked up his menu. "Everything is fine."

"All of the plans for the Daniels Auto retreat have been finalized."

Tyrese smiled in approval. "I shouldn't be surprised. I knew that you wouldn't let any grass grow under your feet once you were back in the office."

"I have to be there a couple of days early, but are you planning on joining us for the weekend?" she asked.

"I'll be there," he responded. "I've cleared my schedule so that I can fly out with you and Max."

Zaire was touched by his thoughtfulness. "You really have my back, don't you?"

Tyrese reached over and took her hand in his own. "I will always have your back, honey."

"Ditto." Zaire picked up her menu.

After lunch, they returned to the office.

"How late do you plan on working today?" she asked. It was almost five-thirty and she did not want to stay much longer.

"Not late at all," Tyrese replied. "This is your first day back, and we're not going to overdo it."

She released a sigh of relief.

"Baby, I am not going to push you further than you are mentally ready to handle. We are going to take this one day at a time. You don't have to be in the office every day. You can work from home whenever you want."

"It's good being back in the office," Zaire told him. "The only time I really feel any angst is in the parking garage." She sat down in the chair facing his desk. "I'm not going to let fear control me."

"I love your spirit."

She gave him a wicked grin. "Is that all you love about me?"

"Definitely not," he responded. "I love everything about you, Zaire."

"If we leave now, we can have the rest of the evening for us," she said quietly. "That is, if you're interested."

Tyrese shut down his computer.

After spending the evening making love, Zaire and Tyrese were awakened by the sound of the telephone ringing.

She answered it. "Hello."

"Sis, it's me," Blaze said. "Natasha's at the hospital. She went into labor. Livi is staying with Joshua, but I'm here at the hospital."

Zaire sat up in bed, pulling the covers up to cover her nakedness. "But it's too soon. The babies aren't due yet." Sage's due date was almost a month before Natasha's— the babies were five weeks early.

Tyrese sat up. "Is everything okay?" he asked in a whisper.

She shrugged her shoulders. "Blaze, I'll be there as soon as I can."

"Mom and Dad are on the way. I haven't called Sage because I don't want her to get upset."

"She's going to be upset, but I don't think she needs to be at the hospital. Sage really needs her rest."

Zaire hung up and climbed out of bed. "Baby, I need to go to the hospital."

Tyrese got up and started to get dressed. "I'll drive you."

"I can have Drayden pick me up. You can go back to sleep."

He shook his head. "I won't be able to sleep with you dealing with this alone."

She looked up at Tyrese. "It's too early for the babies."

"Twins coming early is not unusual," he told her. "Natasha is going to have the best medical care, and the babies will be fine. We have to believe that."

Zaire hugged him. "Thanks for saying that. I needed to hear it."

"Hurry up and get dressed," he told her. "We have to get to the hospital."

Chapter 18

"Why don't you go to bed?" Tyrese suggested when they arrived back at the apartment. They had been at the hospital since midnight. Both babies were breech; Natasha was six centimeters dilated and leaking amniotic fluid. The doctor informed Ari that there was no chance of stopping labor and that Natasha would have to deliver as soon as possible through cesarean section.

Zaire sank down on the sofa. "I think I just want to sit here for a while."

He sat down beside her. "It's amazing to see you with your family. I love the way you all support one another. My parents were a lot like that."

She touched his cheek. "You really miss them, don't you?"

Tyrese nodded. "It would have been great to have

them supporting me when I was going through my storms."

"You're not alone anymore," Zaire reminded him. "You have me."

She called to check on Natasha and the babies a few minutes later.

"Natasha's sleeping, and the babies are fine," she told Tyrese. "Ari won't leave the nursery. He doesn't want the babies alone."

"Are you planning to go back to the hospital?" Tyrese asked.

"It will probably be later this evening. I know Sage will be going by to visit Natasha and the twins."

"Call me if you need me to pick you up from the hospital." Tyrese rose to his feet. "I'm going to shower and change. If you decide that you're coming into the office today—let me know. I'll come pick you up."

Zaire shook her head. "Tyrese, I can do this. If I decide to go to the office, I will drive myself. I can do this."

He wore a look of concern. "Honey, I don't want you to rush into this. I don't mind driving you wherever you need to go, or I can send a car for you."

Zaire gave him a sharp look. "Tyrese, I love you, but I want my life back. I want to be completely free, and I won't be if I can't get behind the wheel of my car and drive to work or anywhere else."

Zaire was not only driving to work, but parking in a well-lit parking spot designated for her near the newly restructured security office. She and Tyrese had driven separately most of the week as he resumed his early schedule. Zaire didn't plan to come in until two hours later.

After a week had passed, Zaire prepared a special dinner on the table to celebrate this recent milestone.

Tyrese came home shortly after eight.

He greeted her with a kiss. "How was your day?"

"Great," Zaire responded. "What about yours?"

"It was busy, but I got a lot of work done."

"Well, tonight I don't want you thinking about work," she told him. "We are going to celebrate."

He smiled. "What are we celebrating, sweetheart?"

"How about the fact that I am completely free from the terrors of my attack," Zaire announced. "I am no longer a victim. Go upstairs and shower. I have something on the bed for you to slip into."

His eyebrows rose in surprise. "Oh, really?"

"Just do what I tell you. I promise it will be worth it."

Tyrese grinned. "I'll be right back."

He returned fifteen minutes later to the candlelit dining room, freshly showered and dressed in the pair of silk pajama pants she had laid out for him.

The soft lighting caressed his complexion, giving it a smooth, creamy texture.

He kissed her passionately.

Zaire reluctantly pulled away. "We'd better eat before the food gets cold."

He groaned, "If you say so—but we could take it to the bedroom with us. I'm just saying...."

Grinning, Zaire slowly untied her robe, displaying a beautiful red silk teddy. "But then you'd ruin the evening I have in mind. There's only one thing I have in mind when it comes to the bedroom."

He sat down at the table. "Let's eat quickly."

She laughed. "Baby, I don't want you choking down your food. We have all night."

Although Zaire's hunger had been sated, her appetite for Tyrese was insatiable. Her breathing quickened at the sight of him licking his full, sexy lips. She had to mentally shake herself in order to concentrate on her dinner.

Zaire had planned to serve dessert, but the truth was that she had other things on her mind. She rose fluidly from her chair, removed her robe and then let it trail behind her as she headed to the master bedroom. Her hips swayed seductively from left to right as she walked.

Tyrese got up and followed her.

Inside the room, he traced a trail of scalding kisses along the rapid pulsation on her throat while his hand set out on a journey of intimate discovery. Zaire could read the promise of delicious magic in his eyes. She felt the fire spreading through every fiber of her being until fervent desire pounded in rhythm with her thundering heart.

Obsessed with the feel of each other's hands and lips, the two fell back on the bed. Zaire's arms slid over Tyrese's sinewy shoulders to hold him close.

Passion streamed through her like a river, sweeping her into a whirlpool of inexpressible splendor. The ever-changing, ever-growing sensations consumed her mind, body and soul.

Their energy spent, Tyrese and Zaire lay entwined.

Feeling more content than she had ever felt in her life, Zaire smiled tenderly.

Gazing into her eyes, Tyrese kissed her softly. "You are my life, Zaire. I don't know what I'd do if I ever lost you."

"You've shown me what it's like to be completely loved by a man. There's nothing or no one who could ever make me abandon what I have with you." Zaire meant it with her entire being.

They showered together, then dressed in robes and went downstairs to have dessert.

Tyrese nodded. "You really outdid yourself tonight. I can't believe that you cooked all of this and baked a cake."

"Okay, I confess," Zaire said. "I didn't bake the cake. Ryan did."

Tyrese laughed. "I knew it."

"No, you didn't," she countered. "How did you know? It's not like I had an empty box of cake mix in the garbage can."

"No, you didn't," he agreed. "But there wasn't any evidence of anything for the cake."

"You went looking for proof that I'd made the cake?" she asked. Zaire couldn't believe he would go through their trash bin just to prove or disprove her cake-baking skills.

"I wasn't looking for proof of anything," he said. "I

just happened to notice it." Setting his champagne flute on the table, Tyrese added, "I could care less whether or not you can bake. I love you regardless."

She reached out across the table, lacing his fingers with her own. "I'm ready to go back to bed. What about you?"

He rose to his feet in response.

Zaire led him back to the bedroom.

They got in bed and snuggled close.

Burying her face against the corded muscles of his chest, Zaire murmured, "What I'm feeling is so extraordinary, it defies description."

Running his fingers through her hair, Tyrese asked, "Now, why is that?"

"Well, I have this incredible man that I love with all of my heart and who loves me back. I'm so excited about our upcoming trip to New York. It's going to be nice exploring the Big Apple with you."

"That's why I wanted to fly in early. Pilar's planning to keep us pretty busy with all of the prewedding celebrations, but I want to spend some quality time with you. Pilar thinks we're flying in on Friday morning."

"You didn't want to tell her that we'd be there on Wednesday?" Zaire inquired.

"No," Tyrese responded. "Trust me. She'd try to put me to work if she knew that we were coming in early."

"What if she calls you?"

"She won't be able to reach me."

Zaire was surprised by his response.

"Actually, I told her that I would be out of town for

a couple of days before the wedding. I just didn't tell her that I would be in New York."

Zaire laughed. "Honey, Pilar knows you very well. She's booked a hotel suite for us from Wednesday to Sunday."

"Really?"

"Yeah. She figured that we might want to spend some time alone."

He kissed her. "How long were you going to keep this from me?"

"I wasn't," she said. "I was just waiting for the right time to tell you."

Zaire saw the flicker of desire in Tyrese's eyes and moved closer to him so that they were skin to skin. "I really believe that our meeting was fate. The day you came down to greet me…I felt an instant connection… like we were kindred spirits."

"Yeah, it's a day I'll never forget. I have always wanted a woman who was just as beautiful on the inside as well as the outside. I love the way you carry yourself and the way you go after what you want. We're definitely kindred spirits, sweetheart. There are times when we're down, but we're never out."

She laid her head in the crook of his neck, contented. "You make me feel special, Tyrese."

"That's because you are," he responded.

Zaire lifted her lips to his.

Tyrese kissed her with a tender brushing of his lips that made her smile.

"Our relationship feels solid as a rock," she whispered. "Nothing can shake or break what we have. I don't think I've ever felt so secure."

Tyrese climbed into the limo behind Zaire. They were en route to the airport to board his company plane. Several of his employees were also joining them on the flight to New York for Pilar's wedding.

"I should have put all of the staff on the other plane so that you and I could be alone," he whispered as the limo rolled to a stop in front of the hangar.

"That's not your style," Zaire whispered back. "We're going to have a good time."

He gave her a tight smile. She knew him so well, although there was one thing he was keeping from her— the phone calls he had been receiving. The ones he wished would stop. Tyrese did not like keeping secrets from her, but after all she had been through, he didn't want to upset her with that.

An hour later, they were lined up on the runway for takeoff.

Zaire stole a peek at Max, who grinned and winked. She awarded him a smile before returning her attention to her iPad.

As soon as they were in the air, a continental breakfast was served.

Tyrese was going over some things with his assistant, so Zaire used the time to catch up on her reading. She glanced over at Max. He had his laptop open, and he appeared to be working on something.

"Max, shut down your computer and relax," she

told him. "We have everything in target. Just enjoy the flight."

He gave her a smile of gratitude.

"You're making me look like a slave driver," Tyrese whispered when he returned to his seat beside her.

"I don't think so," she said. "Everyone knows how dedicated you are to the success of your company. There's nothing wrong with that. If I had as many clients as you—I'd probably be the same way."

"VIP Client Services is just starting out," Tyrese replied. "In six months, you will be looking to hire more staff."

Halfway through the flight, lunch was served.

Zaire fell asleep shortly after she'd finished eating.

The flight attendant brought a light blanket and a pillow for her. While she slept, Tyrese worked on his computer.

He was keeping another secret from Zaire, but this one made him smile. Tyrese reached into his pocket and pulled out a tiny black box. He wanted their trip to New York to be memorable.

"I love everything about New York," Zaire declared the next day as she packed away her purchases. "Even this cold February weather. But I especially love the shopping."

"You're very good at it," Tyrese commented. "In fact, if they were giving out belts—you would be a black belt and your credit card a lethal weapon. You have pulling it out down to a skilled level."

She laughed. "If you think I'm good, you should see Sage at work."

Tyrese walked over to the huge window in their hotel suite and stared out. "I find myself looking for those glorious twin towers every time I'm here." He shook his head sadly. "I lost a couple of good friends."

Zaire walked up and hugged him from behind. "I don't think we will ever forget that day."

"We should never forget," Tyrese said. "I almost joined the military after it happened, but Pilar talked me out of it."

"I'm glad she did," Zaire said. "I think men who are soldiers are brave and courageous, but I could not be married to one. I can't handle giving Uncle Sam that much control over my life, or having to pray for my husband's safety. I've lost two cousins since 9/11."

Tyrese turned around to face her. "I'm sorry."

"If you had gone through with your decision to join, then I never would've met you."

He grinned. "And you wouldn't be the luckiest woman alive."

"I love that you're so humble, baby."

They settled down in the living room area of the suite.

"I'm kind of surprised that we haven't heard from Pilar," Tyrese said.

"She's giving us these couple of days like we wanted," Zaire explained. "Now, tomorrow…you're all hers. You are giving her away and fulfilling all of the duties of a father of the bride."

"She's really sad about her father not being here."

"When did he pass away?" Zaire asked.

"Last year," Tyrese responded. "Pilar was really close to him, and she took his death hard."

"I'm glad that she had you to help her through it."

"She and her mother have a closer relationship now, and that's a good thing."

Zaire laid her head on his chest.

"Why don't you take a nap?" Tyrese suggested. "I know that you must be tired from all of the shopping."

"You think you're so funny." Zaire tossed a pillow in his direction. "However, I am going to take a power nap so that I can be rested before dinner and the play. This will be the first Broadway production I've ever seen."

Tyrese was surprised. "Really?"

She nodded. "I'm from Aspen, Georgia. We didn't come all the way up to New York to watch a play on Broadway. My first visit to the Big Apple was a high school graduation present from my parents. We came up and did a bunch of sightseeing tours, but never saw anything other than the theater on the outside. My parents were about to have three kids in college and one in grad school. Blaze had just graduated with his master's."

"I'd like to visit your hometown one day," he said. "I don't think I'd ever heard of it until it was mentioned in the papers after your father received his inheritance."

"Most people hadn't heard of it," Zaire replied. "Aspen is beautiful, with lots of tree-lined streets, sidewalks with children playing jump rope or shooting marbles. The smell of magnolias in the air…" She closed her eyes for a moment. "I miss seeing our neighbors sitting on their porches drinking lemonade or cola if it's a really hot day."

"Aspen sounds like a Norman Rockwell painting."

Zaire smiled. "I guess it does. It is a beautiful town."

"Sounds like the perfect place to go when you're looking for peace and quiet."

"I thought about going back to Aspen after the attack, but I didn't want to run away because I probably would not have come back to Los Angeles."

"Then I would have come looking for you in Aspen."

"Yeah, right," she uttered. "You were still in denial of your feelings for me."

"I would've come for you, Zaire."

"Well, we will never have to worry about that." She planted a quick kiss on his lips. "I'm off to take that power nap now. I'll see you in about an hour."

Chapter 19

Pilar had chosen to get married at the Loeb Boathouse at Central Park, a popular spot to get married in New York. It was one of the places Tyrese had considered when he was going to get engaged before his life took a turn for the worse.

"This is where the ceremony will be held," Pilar said as they entered a huge room with windows overlooking the lake. "What do you think?"

He smiled. "It's perfect for you."

She surveyed his face. "Tyrese, is everything okay?"

"Yeah."

"I know you," Pilar replied as she ran a hand through her curling tendrils. "There's something that's been bothering you for a while. Does this have to do with—"

"She calls me from time to time, but I hang up. I've changed my number twice."

Pilar's eyes flashed in anger. "You need to let me handle her, Tyrese. I keep telling you—"

"Eventually, she will become bored."

"It's been five years. Why does she want to talk now? Maybe it's because she was kicked to the curb by her husband."

Tyrese's eyebrows rose in surprise. "They're divorced?"

Pilar nodded. "He is married to another woman now. Why? Do you still have feelings for her?"

"No, I love Zaire," Tyrese responded. "I'm just surprised. I never thought he would let her go—it was clear that he loved her."

"She probably couldn't keep her legs closed." Pilar glanced over at Tyrese. "I'm sorry—I shouldn't have said that."

He shrugged.

"Zaire still doesn't know about the calls?"

"I'm not going to upset her with this. In fact, I plan on asking her to marry me tonight."

Pilar broke into a grin. "That's wonderful."

"I'm going to take her on a boat ride after the rehearsal dinner and propose."

She hugged him. "I'm so happy for you. Zaire is perfect for you."

"I'm glad you approve," Tyrese replied with a short chuckle.

Pilar looped her arm through his. "C'mon—let me show you where the reception will be held."

The wedding rehearsal was a comedy of errors, but mostly because the bridal party was playing around. Thankfully, the pastor who was conducting the ceremony had a great sense of humor. Zaire soon realized that he was Pilar's cousin.

After the rehearsal, the groom's parents ushered everyone into a room down the hall where they would have dinner.

Tyrese had generously provided a choice of Broadway or concert tickets to his staff. Max and some of the younger employees opted to see Alicia Keys in concert, while the others decided to see the musical.

While everyone took a seat, the groom's parents remained standing.

Pilar's future father-in-law smiled at everyone and said, "Let us first honor the bride and groom for a moment. To my son, Marshall—your selfless spirit and your loving personality have won you a special gift, your bride, Pilar. May you forever cherish her. Pilar, you are indeed a gift from above, and we welcome you into our family with all our hearts, and we give thanks to our son's good fortune that he found you."

When it was Tyrese's turn to give the toast, he said, "Let us raise our glasses and toast the happy couple. If her father were here, he would be doing this." He looked to his right. "Mrs. Millbrook, would you stand with me?"

Pilar's mother rose to her feet.

"Pilar is like a sister to me. Her mother is my other mother, so it gives me great pleasure to share in this part of her journey as Pilar begins a new life with Marshall, who will love, honor and protect her. Pilar, I want you to know that even though he is not here, your father will always be with you in spirit. Cheers."

Zaire took a sip of her champagne.

"That was really sweet," she whispered when Tyrese sat back down beside her.

After dinner, Tyrese took Zaire down to the lake, where a number of rustic, shacklike buildings served as boathouses. "This is so beautiful at night," Zaire murmured as she stared out a huge window. "I can see why she wanted to have the wedding at sunset. The view is going to be spectacular."

Tyrese agreed, "We hosted an event here and I fell in love with this place at that time. In fact, that's when Pilar met Marshall. It was love at first sight for them."

"It's worked out well for them," Zaire responded. "Tomorrow evening, they will be man and wife."

"I would say it's worked out just as well for us," Tyrese announced.

Zaire met his gaze.

Tyrese smiled at her. "Sweetheart, I love you so much, and I want to spend the rest of my life with you."

She gasped in surprise at the sight of the tiny velvet box in his hand.

"Will you marry me?"

Zaire gasped in surprise. "Tyrese, this is for real?"

He laughed. "Baby, it's for real. I want you to be my wife. I want to protect you for the rest of your life. I never want you to feel scared ever again."

She hugged him. "I love you so much, Tyrese."

"Then tell me if you're going to be my wife."

"Definitely," she said. "I will marry you, Tyrese. You are the only man I want to grow old with."

Tyrese placed the ring, a four-carat cushion-cut ruby with channel-set diamonds on each side, on her finger. "I know how much you love red, so when I saw this ring—I knew it was perfect for you."

"Red is my signature color," she said with a grin. "I can't believe we're getting married."

"It's true, so you might as well get used to the idea."

This was the happiest moment of her life. It was perfect. For the first time in a long time, all the shadows surrounding her heart had finally dissipated. She loved him with her heart, body and soul.

She loved most that he was honest and had never given her pause to wonder if he was keeping anything from her. Zaire did not like secrets.

Tyrese escorted Pilar's mother up to the stage and took the microphone. "Traditionally, this is the time when fathers of the bride have the pleasure of making the first speech. Pilar, when your father realized that he would not be here for your wedding day, he gave me explicit instructions—he wrote down what he would say and he gave me that letter to read to you."

His eyes watered at the sight of Pilar's tears. Out of

"I was going to get through it," Tyrese stated. "I promised her father. When my dad died, he became a surrogate father to me. He was the one who took me to all of my sporting events in high school. He stayed on me about my grades. He helped me with my college applications."

"You loved him."

He nodded.

She reached over and took his hand in her own. "This is just one more reason why I love you. You hold such honor and devotion for the people you care about, Tyrese."

He picked up her hand and kissed it.

Zaire turned to him and said, "I think I have the perfect theme for our wedding. What could be a more romantic wedding theme than celebrating long-lasting love?"

He smiled. "I like it."

"Our theme can be both incredibly sentimental and funny—it's whatever we want it to mean and we can incorporate it in every aspect of our wedding. For example, we can get married in a place where there are forever happy endings and true love never dies."

"Is there such a place?" Tyrese asked.

Zaire nodded. "We can get married at Disneyland in honor of all of the great loves. Mickey and Minnie, Snow White and Prince Charming, Belle and the Beast…"

Tyrese broke into a grin. "You've really given this a lot of thought, I see."

"Pilar's wedding has inspired my creative side."

He kissed her. "I love you so much."

"Ditto."

"Pilar gave me the name of her wedding coordinator, but I'm not sure you are going to need it."

"Max is actually going to be our coordinator. He and I talked about it while you all were taking pictures before the wedding."

"I forgot he used to be an event planner, and I think he's worked with a wedding coordinator in the past."

"He has," Zaire confirmed. "Tyrese, I don't know about you, but I'm so excited about starting our life together."

"I've been thinking that you should move into the house with me. I'll buy out your lease."

"Really?"

He nodded. "Unless you'd rather not live with me until after the wedding."

"If you don't mind, I think I'd like to move in with one of my siblings until the wedding. I don't want to move into your home until it becomes *our* home," Zaire said. "I hope you're not disappointed."

"I've gotten used to sleeping beside you at night, but that's fine."

"I didn't say I won't be spending time at the house— I just don't really feel right about moving in until after we're married."

Tyrese glanced around. "I'm going to get something to drink. Do you want anything?"

"A glass of sparkling water," Zaire said. "Thanks, babe."

He winked at her.

"Tyrese..."

He turned around. "What are you doing here?" The shock of seeing his ex-girlfriend after all these years hit him full force.

"I came to town on business, and then I heard about Pilar's wedding. I knew you would be here, so I extended my trip. Ty, I know that a lot has happened between us, but we really need to talk."

"Kennedy, there's nothing we need to discuss. Now, if you will excuse me..." He attempted to step around her, but she blocked his path.

"Tyrese, I am divorced," she announced. "There was no way I could stay with Ross after what he did to you."

"I heard that *he* was the one who kicked *you* to the curb. Regardless of what really happened between you and Ross, I really don't care. That man ruined my life because of you."

"Ty, I'm so sorry about that," she told him. "But look at you now. You have your own company and it's exploding. Can we please go somewhere and talk? There's so much I need to tell you—"

"I'm engaged," he interjected, cutting off her words.

He heard her quick intake of breath.

"Kennedy, we have nothing to talk about, so please stay away from me. Don't call me anymore. Just do me a favor and leave me alone, please."

"What we shared was special, Ty. I never told you about Ross because I was going to leave him for you. *I was leaving him.*"

"You were never honest with me, Kennedy. I could never trust you again."

To Tyrese's surprise, she showed no reaction.

"I need to get back to my fiancée."

Tyrese walked away without one look back.

"I was about to come looking for you," Zaire told him when he returned to the table. "What took you so long?"

"I ran into someone I used to know." Tyrese stole a quick peek over his shoulder. Kennedy was standing near one of the exit doors, watching him.

He turned his attention to Zaire.

She scanned his face. "You okay?"

He put on a tight smile and nodded. "I'm fine, baby."

Tyrese pulled at the collar of his tuxedo shirt.

"Do you mind if I whisk your fiancée to the dance floor?" Max asked.

"Not at all," Tyrese responded with a smile.

"Did I just see Kennedy here?" Pilar asked as she sat down in the seat Zaire had just vacated.

He gave a slight nod. "She keeps telling me that we need to talk. Why, I don't know—there is nothing to say."

"She's stalking you, Tyrese." Pilar glanced over her shoulder. "If I see her again, I'm going to have security throw her out. I can't believe she showed up at my wedding uninvited."

"I don't want her anywhere near Zaire."

"Have you told her about Kennedy?" Pilar asked.

Tyrese nodded. "Of course. I just don't want her up-setting Zaire. She's happy and I want her to stay that way."

"Tyrese, tell me what happened earlier," Zaire said when they returned to their hotel suite. "Something upset you, and I know it. What's going on?"

He sat down on the sofa beside her. "I saw the woman from my past. According to her, she just happened to be in town and heard about Pilar's wedding."

Zaire was shocked. "She came to the wedding? *Uninvited?*"

"She was at the reception," he responded. "I don't know if she attended the wedding ceremony."

She looked him in the eye. "Tyrese, why didn't you tell me?"

"I didn't want to upset you."

"You didn't think I could handle meeting your ex-girlfriend?" Zaire accused. "I'm really not that fragile."

"Honey, I know that you are not—" His voice broke off in midsentence. "I'm sorry."

"So what did she want? I mean, you haven't heard from her in all this time."

Tyrese did not respond.

"She's been calling you?" Zaire inquired.

"I've asked her to stop," he responded. "She keeps saying that we need to talk. I've told her that there is nothing to discuss."

"But she's not taking no for an answer, I suppose."

"She wanted me to know that she's divorced. It doesn't matter to me one way or the other. I did tell her that I was engaged."

Zaire smiled. "You did?"

He nodded. "I don't want anything else to do with her."

"Tyrese, please don't keep anything like this from me ever again," she stated. "You said we were a team. I have never liked secrets." Zaire reached over and took his hand in her own. "After my attack, you said that we could get through anything as long as we were together. I believed you."

"I meant every word of it," Tyrese assured her. "There will never be any more secrets between us. I give you my word."

Chapter 20

Zaire and Tyrese drove out to Pacific Palisades the following weekend for the family cookout. She was looking forward to seeing her brand-new niece. Sage and Ryan were over the moon since the birth of their daughter three weeks ago.

Sage pointed to Zaire's hand as soon as they entered the house. "Okay, you want to tell us about the rock on your finger? I can see it all the way over here."

Smiling, she glanced over at Tyrese. "What do you think?"

He grinned. "I think they already have an idea."

Holding up her hand, Zaire announced, "We're engaged."

"That's wonderful news," Barbara exclaimed. "I have

to say that I'm not a bit surprised, though. I saw this coming the first time Tyrese came to the house."

"Knock knock…"

They turned to find Harold standing in the doorway holding a bouquet of flowers and a bottle of wine.

"Harold, come on in," Barbara said with a smile. "You're just in time. Zaire and Tyrese just announced their engagement."

He gave them a genuine grin. "The family just keeps getting bigger and bigger. That's a good thing. Congrats."

Zaire surprised Harold by giving him a hug. "It's good to see you, cousin."

He walked over to Barbara and gave her the flowers. "I hope that you don't mind, but I brought someone with me."

Looking past him, Barbara asked, "Where is she?"

"She's outside talking to Livi and Blaze."

"Is it Amy?" Zaire inquired.

Harold nodded.

Zaire bit back her smile. She recalled that he and Amy had spent most of the evening talking and dancing at Livi and Blaze's wedding reception.

Barbara escorted Harold to the patio, where Malcolm was heating up the grill.

"Is there something I'm missing?" Tyrese asked. "Who is Amy?"

"Livi's friend," Zaire responded. "They met when Livi and Blaze got married."

Just then, Livi and Amy walked inside, laughing and talking.

"That's Amy?"

Zaire smiled and nodded. "I think Harold's got a thing for her. They make a cute couple. I just hope he won't hurt her."

Harold's sister arrived with her fiancé.

"Is that my brother's car out there?" Meredith asked.

"Yes," Sage responded as she laid the sleeping baby on a blanket someone had spread on the sofa. "He's out back with Dad."

"I'm so glad he decided to come." Meredith glanced over at Amy and waved. "They have been seeing a lot of each other," she whispered.

Zaire found that Harold possessed stellar skills on the basketball court.

When he made his third three-pointer, she yelled, "I see you, Harold. You go—"

"Hey, stop cheering for my opponent," Tyrese told her.

She laughed. "I'm sorry, babe." Zaire put her hands to her mouth. "You go, Tyrese. I see you."

"That's a pity cheer," he complained from across the court.

"No, it isn't," Zaire yelled back.

"Yeah, it was," Sage told her. They were seated next to each other on the newly installed bleachers. Baby Honor was in the house with their mother.

Natasha and Ari joined them.

"Where are the babies?" Zaire asked. "And my little man, Joshua?"

"Christian and Crystal are in the nursery with your mother and my mom," Natasha said. "Joshua is over there with your dad. He wants to learn how to grill."

Natasha glanced down at Zaire's hand. "Oh, my goodness! You're getting married."

Ari took his attention off the game. "Who's getting married?"

"I am," Zaire stated.

"Wow. I didn't know you two were *that* serious. Are you sure you aren't moving too fast?"

She boldly met her brother's gaze. "Ari, I love him and he loves me. Why shouldn't we get married?"

Natasha laughed. "He's just messing with you, Zaire."

"Did you see her?" he asked Natasha. "She was about to take my head off."

Zaire gave him a playful slap on the arm. "I was not. I was just letting you know that when two people love each other the way Tyrese and I do—the next step is marriage. I figured you should know that since you married Natasha."

"I'm really happy for you, sis."

"Thanks, Ari," Zaire responded. "I've never been this happy. It defies all reason."

Natasha nodded in agreement. "I know that feeling well."

Ari embraced his wife and planted a kiss on her forehead.

Zaire smiled as she observed her brother's affection

for his wife. She was looking forward to raising a family with Tyrese and growing old together. In a few short months, she would be his wife.

The next six months flew by, bringing them closer to their wedding day.

Zaire packed up to go home and then stopped by Tyrese's office.

"I'll call you later," Zaire said from the doorway. "I'm meeting Sage and Livi for dinner."

"I'll walk you to your car," Tyrese told her as he pushed away from his desk.

They took the elevator down to the lobby area.

"Have you ordered your tuxedo yet?" Zaire asked as she scanned through a checklist on her iPhone.

Tyrese shook his head. "I'm going by the store on Friday. I'll do it then."

She gave a short, impatient sigh.

He looked puzzled. "What?"

"Babe, we leave on Wednesday for the Daniels Auto retreat. You won't be in town on Friday."

"That's right," he responded. "I'll take care of it tomorrow, sweetheart. I promise."

Zaire gave him a look that clearly said that she didn't believe him at all.

"I will," he insisted. "I will order it tomorrow."

Zaire made a mental note to follow up with Tyrese. He already owned several tuxes, but she wanted a custom one for their wedding. She had spoken with two fashion designers before deciding on the one who would create their wedding attire.

"I hope you're not upset with me."

She kissed him on the lips. "I'm not angry with you, babe. I just need you to get fitted so that we can order your tux."

"I won't let you down, sweetheart. I'll take care of it tomorrow."

Zaire smiled at him. "I know that."

Tyrese waited until she was safely in the car and driving out of the garage before he returned to his office.

He walked into his office to find a woman dressed in black waiting for him.

"Kennedy, what are you doing here?" Tyrese was glad that Zaire had already left the building. "Why won't you just leave me alone?"

"Every time I've tried to talk to you, you hang up on me. Ty, you treated me like dirt in New York. If this was just about me, you would never hear from me again, but it isn't."

"What are you talking about, Kennedy?"

She held up a photograph. "This is about him."

Tyrese felt as if he had been kicked in the gut. "What does this child have to do with me?"

"He's your son," Kennedy announced with a smile. "Yours and mine."

"I don't believe you."

"I found out that I was pregnant right after you left Chicago," she told him. "The truth is that I thought Ross was the father. We found out that he wasn't a couple of years ago when Matt got sick. Ross left me when he found out."

Tyrese shook his head in disbelief. "This can't be happening."

"Ty, we have a child together, and I want you to get to know Matt. He's such a beautiful little boy."

"Kennedy, you are a liar and you will say anything to get what you want. I'm sorry, but I don't believe you."

"Our son is five years old and he needs his father. He needs you."

"I want a paternity test."

She looked offended. "I've already told you that Ross divorced me because Matt is not his son." Kennedy pulled a document out of her purse. "Here are his results. They clearly state that he is not the father."

"I'm getting married."

"Do you really want to go through with a marriage when we have a child together?"

Tyrese couldn't believe what he was hearing. "You can't actually believe that I would leave Zaire for you."

"Maybe you won't do it for me, but what about Matt? He needs you." Kennedy walked over to him. "I still love you so much. I'm sorry for all of the lies, but if you'd give me another chance—"

He cut her off. "No. I don't want anything to do with you. If Matt is my son, then I will be a father to him, but as for you—what we had is over. Zaire is my life."

"How do you think she's going to feel about you having a child with another woman?"

"It happened long before I met her. Zaire and I will work through this situation."

Kennedy shrugged. "I hope that you're right."

"I need some time to digest this news," he stated.

"Okay," she murmured. "I will be out of the country for about a month. This should give you enough time to figure out the best way to handle this situation. I know that you will do the right thing."

When she left, Tyrese sat down at his desk with his hands to his face. He had no idea how he was going to tell Zaire.

Zaire noted that something was going on with Tyrese. He had been quieter than normal for the past couple of days. He had gotten fitted for his tux and the order had been placed, much to her relief.

They were en route to Denver, Colorado, for the Daniels Auto retreat. She reached over and covered his hand with her own. "What's wrong?"

He looked at her. "Nothing. Why do you ask?"

"You look troubled," she responded. "Did something happen that I don't know about? Tyrese, you don't have to keep anything from me. You know how I hate secrets."

"Honey, everything is fine," Tyrese said. "We are getting married soon. This should be our main focus."

"It is," she told him, "but I am worried about you."

Tyrese kissed her. "Don't be. I'm okay."

He was keeping something from her. Zaire was sure of it, but she had no idea of what it could be. She wished that he would confide in her.

Tyrese worked most of the flight to Denver. She moved to sit beside Max to avoid disturbing him.

The plane landed in Denver shortly after ten o'clock. They were whisked by limo to the Willow Creek Ranch.

"I really hope that everything goes well this weekend," Zaire said. "If it does, then Bill is going to sign a five-year contract with us."

Tyrese patted her hand. "It's going to be perfect."

She smiled. "No event is ever really perfect, babe. But I hope to get as close to it as possible."

He still wore that distracted look on his face, which troubled Zaire. She didn't need this right now. She needed to focus on the retreat, making sure that everything went according to plan.

Later, when they checked into their room, Zaire confronted him. "Tyrese, please talk to me. I know that something is going on with you."

"I just have some issues on a project," he said. "Honey, I'm not going to do you any good here. Why don't I fly back to Los Angeles?"

Zaire hid her disappointment. "If that's what you want to do."

"I think it's best," he told her. "If I can get this taken care of quickly—I'll fly back down on Friday."

She folded her arms across her chest. "Okay. Hopefully, I'll see you on Friday."

He wanted desperately to confide in Zaire, but now was not the right time. She was producing her first event, and Tyrese did not want anything to distract her.

He also feared losing Zaire. He knew how she felt about family. She would rather give up her own happiness than keep Tyrese from his own child.

He was still not sure whether Kennedy was telling the truth about Matt. Until he knew without a doubt that the little boy was his son, Tyrese was not going to say anything to Zaire. He would use the next couple of days to get himself together, and then he would fly back to Denver to be with Zaire.

Leaving in the first place had been a mistake, Tyrese realized. He was going to make it up to her. He knew exactly what to do.

Zaire gasped in surprise when she entered her hotel suite. "When did you get here?" she asked Tyrese.

"An hour ago," he responded.

She fell into his arms. "I missed you so much. Why didn't you tell me that you were coming?"

"I wanted to make it a special night for you," Tyrese replied. "I've ordered dinner for us—none of that healthy stuff that you all have been eating all day. We even have chocolate."

She clapped her hands in delight. "Yes…"

He covered her mouth with his, kissing her with his entire being.

Zaire matched him kiss for kiss.

She didn't protest when he picked her up and carried her over to the bed.

Tyrese undressed her and then removed his own clothes.

He joined her beneath the covers.

Zaire clung to him, kissing him passionately as they made love.

Afterward, she lay in his arms. "Dinner was a bust, but at least we still have chocolate."

Tyrese laughed. "If you're hungry, I can order more food."

She shook her head. "I'm fine." Zaire sat up in bed. "I'm glad to see that you're back to your old self, babe. I guess everything worked out the way you wanted it."

"Not really," Tyrese said, "but I'm working on it."

She kissed him. "I'm so glad that you came back. Now it feels like everything is going to work out great."

"I can't wait to marry you," Tyrese stated with a grin. "You know...we don't have to wait. We can get married right away."

She gave him a sidelong look. "What's gotten into you?"

"I'm ready to make you my wife."

"We're getting married in a few weeks," she reminded him. "Everything is all planned."

He met her gaze. "So you want to wait?"

"Yes," she told Tyrese. "I love you and I'm very excited about marrying you, but Max and I have worked hard planning this wedding. It's going to be perfect."

"I know it will," he said. "Because you are going to be my wife."

Chapter 21

The week after the retreat, Zaire and Tyrese joined Harold in France to check out the villa she had suggested for his company's retreat. This was the last business trip she and Tyrese would take before their wedding, which would be in two weeks.

Saint-Tropez was instantly one of Zaire's favorite places to visit. She fell in love with the pink, orange and deep red town houses that framed the flotilla-filled port. "Tyrese, the city is everything that I read it was. I could actually live here."

He smiled. "Is that a hint?"

"No," she responded. "I just think it's beautiful and picturesque. I'm sure it inspires artists from all over."

They walked hand in hand along the waterfront.

"Are you ready to head back to the hotel?" Tyrese asked. "We're meeting Harold for lunch in an hour."

"Can we stop at this shop for a moment?"

Tyrese looked down at the four bags in his left hand. "You don't think we've done enough shopping already?"

"We can get an early start on Christmas shopping this year."

He kissed her. "Anything you want, sweetheart."

Zaire took a few photographs of interesting studios and historical structures. Her favorite was the Musée de l'Annonciade.

They headed back to the hotel.

Harold was already seated and looking through the menu when they arrived.

"How long have you been waiting?" Zaire asked.

"Not long," he responded with a warm smile. "I hope that you two enjoyed your sightseeing."

"You should have joined us." Zaire picked up her menu.

"I didn't want to intrude."

"Harold, you're family. You are not intruding."

She glanced around the dining area and smiled. "I love the decor."

Tyrese glanced up. "It is nice."

When their food arrived, Zaire announced, "The food smells delicious. I sound like a tourist, don't I?"

Tyrese and Harold both laughed.

"Well, I *am* a tourist. This is my first trip to France, but it definitely won't be my last. I love it here in Saint-Tropez."

Tyrese agreed.

"Harold, I hope that you don't mind my asking, but are you and Amy dating?" Zaire wondered.

He looked at her. "We are exploring the concept."

Zaire laughed. "I like the way you put that." She held up a hand. "You can relax. I won't ask any more questions."

"It's fine. I really like Amy, and we are just taking it one day at a time."

"She seems really nice," Zaire said.

After lunch, Harold announced, "I'm going to meet up with a friend I went to college with. We can meet for breakfast tomorrow morning if you'd like."

"That's fine," Zaire replied. "Have fun."

"So what are we going to do now?" Tyrese asked as they took the elevator to the floor they were staying on.

"I have an idea. We can…" She leaned over to whisper in his ear.

"I'm right behind you."

"When I was growing up, I always dreamed of going to Disneyland or Disney World—it didn't matter which," Tyrese said. "My parents couldn't afford it. The first time I ever came out here was for a special event."

Zaire embraced him. "I love you so much."

"You have given me a reason to live, sweetheart. My life has taken on new meaning since the day you walked into 640 San Vincente."

"Tomorrow, you will be my husband. We will have

our happily ever after." She broke into a grin. "I can't wait to marry you."

"We can always elope," Tyrese suggested.

"My parents would probably kill us both if we ran off and got married," she told him. "Look, this is Mickey's house."

"I love seeing you so happy," he said with a grin.

She surveyed his face. "You know, you could look a little more excited at the thought of my being your wife."

There were times when Zaire thought she detected something intense in Tyrese's gaze, but she could not be sure. Perhaps there was something still going on at work. He did not seem to want to discuss whatever it was with her. He was a private man, and she realized that there were some things he would never share with her.

"Everyone should be checking into the hotel right about now," Tyrese announced.

"You want to head over there?" she asked.

He nodded. "I need to make some calls before our rehearsal."

Zaire shifted her purse from one side to the other. "I probably need to check in with Max."

They left the park.

Tyrese stole a peek at her. He hoped that she did not suspect anything. He needed to make sure his security staff kept Kennedy Lassiter away from his wedding as well as any members of the media. She was due back in town any day now. He had not heard from Kennedy since the day she'd come to M.G., but she knew that he had planned to go through with his wedding to Zaire. He did not put anything past Kennedy.

After the wedding, he would tell Zaire everything.

Zaire woke up early the morning of her wedding. She climbed out of bed and walked over to where her wedding gown was hanging. The cap sleeves, lace, embroidery, pearl beads and rhinestone embellishments made the dress perfect for the type of wedding Zaire had in mind. She wanted to look like a princess.

She ran her fingers across the beading and smiled. In a few hours, she would be Mrs. Tyrese Moore.

"What are you doing up so early?"

Zaire turned around to face her mother. She and her parents were sharing a two-bedroom suite. "I couldn't sleep another minute. I'm too excited, Mama."

Barbara smiled. "I was the same way when I married your father."

"Mama, how did you know that Daddy was the man for you?"

"When I found myself wanting to be his partner in good times and bad," Barbara said. "We went through something right before we got married that would have probably made another woman question her decision to get married, but for me it was a no-brainer. I was going to stand by my man.

"We're going to order breakfast. What would you like to eat?"

"Just some toast and scrambled eggs," she responded. "I'm not really hungry."

"Honey, you don't want to pass out. You have a long day ahead of you."

"I'll have a nice lunch," she promised. Zaire picked up her phone. "I need to check in with Max. I'll meet you and Daddy in the dining room."

Tyrese stared out of the window of his hotel suite. He was in the honeymoon suite, and tonight he would not be alone. His wife would be staying with him. Although they had not said their vows yet, he felt as though Zaire was already his wife.

He was ready to get the wedding festivities over with. A wave of apprehension swept through Tyrese as he thought of Kennedy.

Tyrese was suddenly filled with guilt. It had been wrong for him to keep this secret from Zaire. He had to tell her now, before they got married. He owed her the truth.

The ringing cell phone cut into his turbulent thoughts.

He sighed with relief when he saw that the caller was Pilar.

"Hello."

"What are you doing?" she asked.

"Having a cup of coffee," Tyrese responded. "What are *you* doing?"

"Marshall and I just came back from the gym. We had a great workout. Are you okay?" she asked him. "You don't sound like yourself."

Pilar knew him well.

"Hey, can you come to my room for a minute?" Tyrese asked. "I really need to talk to you. It's about Kennedy."

"I'll be right there."

Pilar knocked on his door a few minutes later.

"Please tell me that you do not still have feelings for that woman," Pilar said when she entered the suite.

"No. I want to marry Zaire. I'm very clear on this."

Pilar was confused. "Then what does this have to do with Kennedy?"

"She has a child," Tyrese announced. "Kennedy says that the child is mine, Pilar. What am I going to do?"

"Have a paternity test, for one thing," she uttered.

"She says that Ross divorced her because he found out that the child wasn't his."

Pilar shook her head in disbelief. "I'm not buying it."

"I haven't told Zaire anything about this and I feel really guilty about it."

"Tyrese…"

He paced back and forth. "I just couldn't bring myself to tell her that I may have fathered a child. But I can't keep a secret like this from the woman I'm about to marry. I need to tell her the truth."

"This is your wedding day, Tyrese. Do you really want to tell her something like this before you get married?"

His gaze met hers. "Wouldn't you want to know?"

"If it were true, I would say yes," Pilar responded.

"But I don't think that it is—just wait until after the wedding, Tyrese. Don't ruin this day for her."

"I don't want to lose her, Pilar."

"Zaire loves you. She will forgive you, Tyrese."

"I hope you're right, Pilar."

Chapter 22

Zaire's dream wedding had become a reality. She sniffed the fragrant scent of her wedding bouquet as she rode in the Crystal Coach to the Sleeping Beauty Castle where the ceremony would be held.

She felt like a princess on the way to marry her prince. It was a perfect day for a wedding.

Her father and bridal party greeted her in the forecourt of the castle.

Zaire could hear the harpist playing in the background. The celestial tones reverberated throughout, adding to the romantic ambience of the moment. She looked up at her father and smiled.

"You look beautiful, baby girl."

"Thank you, Daddy." Zaire glanced at Livi. "I'm getting married."

Sage adjusted the straps of her gown. "You won't be getting married if you don't get inside to the ceremony. It's time."

The bridal party lined up for the processional.

Zaire held on to her father's arm. "This is it, Daddy. I'm about to embark on a new journey."

He kissed her cheek. "You have a good man in Tyrese. Never forget that."

"I won't."

Herald trumpeters proclaimed her arrival with commanding and triumphant sounds. Zaire thought they would add a touch of sophistication and fanfare to her ceremony.

Her eyes grew wet with tears at the sight of Tyrese. He looked so handsome in the military-style tuxedo. It was one befitting a royal—her Prince Charming.

Zaire couldn't take her eyes off him.

A tear escaped one eye when her father placed her hand in Tyrese's. She was ready to become a wife, but a part of her was saddened that she was no longer her father's little girl.

When the pastor asked, "Is there anyone who objects to this union?" Zaire couldn't help but wonder why it was still a part of most ceremonies. Who would actually stand up and do something like—

"I do."

Shock flew through Zaire's body at the response. She and Tyrese both turned to face their guests.

A woman with honey-blond tresses stood up and

eased into the aisle. She looked at Tyrese as she approached them.

Her eyes moved and stayed on Zaire. "I'm sorry, but I couldn't let this marriage happen without you knowing the truth."

"This is not the time," Tyrese said in a low voice.

Zaire looked at Tyrese, noting the fury blazing in his eyes. "Who is she?"

"Kennedy Lassiter."

"She's the one from your past," Zaire stated.

Tyrese gave a slight nod.

"So he's told you about me," Kennedy said, a smile tugging at her lips.

Zaire looked her straight in the face and asked, "What do you want from us?"

"I don't want anything from *you*," she replied smugly. "Tyrese knows why I'm here. He and I need to talk."

"Since you decided to make a scene, why don't you just say whatever you have to say," he told her. "You can say it in front of my wife."

Kennedy gave a short laugh. "She is not your wife yet."

"She will be soon enough."

"Young lady, it's time for you to leave," Franklin said as he walked toward Kennedy.

"Please get her out of here," Zaire said. "And make sure she stays away from our reception."

"Don't you dare touch me," Kennedy spat, taking a step back from Franklin. "I will not be dismissed any longer. Tyrese, you've given me no choice." Her gaze traveled to Zaire. "Your soon-to-be husband and I have a son together. There are things that we need to discuss concerning our child."

Zaire's mouth dropped open in utter shock. For a moment, it seemed as if the room were spinning. She was vaguely aware of Sage taking her bouquet while Tyrese supported her frame.

"What did you just say?" she sputtered. "What game are you playing?"

"Ty and I have a son," Kennedy repeated. "I thought you should know."

Zaire glanced at Tyrese. "Did you know about this?"

"She told me a few weeks ago, but I don't believe her. I—"

Before he could finish his sentence, Zaire broke into a sprint down the aisle.

Tyrese glared at Kennedy. "Do you enjoy ruining my life?"

"I'm not trying to ruin your life. I just want my son to have both of his parents."

"We need to have that paternity test done as soon as possible."

"For what?" she asked. "I know that you're Matt's father."

"I have to check on Zaire," he said, brushing past Kennedy.

She grabbed his arm. "Matt and I need you," she said.

Tyrese gave her a hard stare. "I'm going to check on my wife."

"She is not your wife."

"Go check on my sister," Sage said. "I'll keep Miss Lassiter occupied."

Zaire wiped her eyes with the handkerchief her mother had given her before the wedding. She jumped at the sound of the knock on the door.

Barbara opened the door and stuck her head inside. "Can I come in?"

She nodded.

She sat down beside her daughter. "How are you holding up?"

"I just found out that my fiancé has a son. I'm doing okay for the most part, don't you think?"

"You're handling this very well, but I'm not surprised," Barbara stated. "You are a strong young woman."

"I'm also mad as hell."

Barbara chuckled. "That's my girl."

"I wanted to be the mother of his first child." Zaire sighed softly. "It's not the child's fault, though."

"No, it isn't. That little boy has nothing to do with what happened."

"What type of woman does this?" Zaire asked. "Why would she wait and do something like this at our wedding? But the real question is why didn't Tyrese tell me about this? I knew something had been bothering him, but he would never talk about it."

"I'm ready to discuss it now."

Zaire glanced over her shoulder. Tyrese was standing in the doorway.

"I never should have kept this from you."

"You're right about that," she snapped.

Barbara reached over and patted Zaire's arm. "Hear him out," she whispered, and then she rose to her feet. "I'll leave you two alone to talk."

She paused at the door and said, "I'll have the harpist play a few selections to keep the guests entertained."

Tyrese sat down beside her. "Honey, I'm so sorry."

"Why didn't you tell me?" Zaire demanded. "How could you let her blindside me like that?"

"I was going to tell you after the wedding. I didn't mention it before because I wanted to have a paternity test done, but she's been out of the country. Zaire, I love you. I want you to be my wife."

"I love you, too. However, there is something else we have to discuss."

"The child."

"Your son," Zaire corrected. "Do you believe her?"

"I don't know what to believe."

"Why did she wait this long to tell you, Tyrese?"

"I don't know." He looked at her. "What happens now?"

"I wish I had an answer for you, Tyrese, but I don't."

"I don't want to lose you."

"You have a lot to consider right now," Zaire told him. "I know that you love me, but you have just found out that you have a son. You need to deal with that first. He is your priority."

"So what are you saying?" he wanted to know. "Are you calling off the wedding?"

"I think it's best for now."

Tyrese shook his head sadly. "I can't believe this is happening."

"This is certainly not the way I thought my wedding would turn out."

Tyrese rose to his feet. "I guess we need to make some sort of announcement."

"I can't go back in there right now," Zaire stated. "I think I'm just going to go back to my parents' house."

"Can I come see you later?"

"Sure, but Tyrese…you need to meet your son and spend some time with him."

Zaire allowed her tears to flow after he'd walked out of the room.

"Surely, you are not going to just let this woman win?"

She looked up to find Franklin standing in the doorway. "Tyrese has a child with her. I can't compete with that."

"He loves you and you love him. Together you can get through anything, including this."

Zaire wiped her eyes. "He needs time to deal with this new role."

"You can give him that as his wife," Franklin countered. "Besides, it might be wise to have a paternity test done before you toss him over to that young lady."

She gave him a sidelong glance. "You don't think she's lying, do you?"

Franklin shrugged. "It's been done many times over the years. I just saw Tyrese, and this man is heartbroken because he believes that he's lost you."

"He hasn't lost me," Zaire responded. "I'm going to stand by my man."

"Then touch up your makeup and prove it to him."

Zaire rushed back to the castle and walked inside the room where everyone was gathered. She saw Tyrese standing up front. She frowned when she saw Kennedy seated in the third row, watching him expectantly. Zaire itched to tear the smile off the woman's face.

"Thank you all for coming," Tyrese began. "In light of all that just transpired, Zaire and I have decided to—"

"Proceed with our wedding ceremony," she finished for him. Smiling, Zaire walked down the aisle to join him up front.

Kennedy rose to her feet and stepped in the aisle, blocking Zaire's path. She stood with her arms folded across her chest and said, "You can't force him into going through with this wedding."

Zaire met her gaze straight on. "Kennedy, I don't know what game you are playing, but it is not going to work. Tyrese and I are still getting married."

Kennedy looked at Tyrese. "You still plan on getting married? Your son deserves two full-time parents."

"If he is my son, I intend to be there for him," Tyrese explained. "Zaire is going to be my wife and his stepmother."

Kennedy shook her head. "Oh, no—I'm not letting her anywhere near my child. If you marry that woman, you will never see your son."

"That's where you are wrong, Kennedy. He's going to see his child," Zaire interjected. "Even if it means going to court. But first we are having a paternity test performed. We want proof that Tyrese fathered your son."

"Who do you think you are?" Kennedy demanded. "You don't have a thing to do with this."

"He's the man I'm going to marry, and this gives me the right," she countered. "Although you were not on our guest list, you are welcome to stay here. After all, every fairy-tale romance has to have a wicked witch lingering around somewhere."

Her words brought laughter from her guests and a flash of anger from Kennedy.

"Or I can have security escort you out."

"Tyrese…" Kennedy pleaded. "Don't do this…."

"Okay, we'll do it your way," Zaire stated. "Franklin, would you escort Miss Lassiter out of the park?"

She walked up to Tyrese and asked, "Do you still want to marry me?"

He grinned. "More than ever."

The guests applauded as they took their places.

* * *

Mickey Mouse and Minnie strolled around the room taking pictures with guests. Snow White and Prince Charming joined them, as well. Zaire looked up at her husband and smiled. The wedding had not gone exactly the way she had planned, but she had no regrets.

They sat down at the bridal table as her father walked up to the stage to speak.

"I suppose that after thirty-eight years of happy marriage I ought to be able to come up with something meaningful to say. Tyrese, just remember these two words...*all* and *only.* You will hear them time and again. Such as, *all* you need to do is...it *only* costs so much. And especially this one—it will *only* take five minutes. These are all gross understatements, but someone once said that women are to be loved and not understood. Marriage is the meeting of two minds, of two hearts and of two souls. It became pretty clear today that Tyrese and Zaire are a perfect example of this. May they be blessed with happiness that grows and with love that lasts and a peaceful life together. My prayer is enjoyment for today, the fulfillment of all their hopes and dreams for tomorrow and love and happiness always."

"I want to thank you for marrying me today," Tyrese told her as they danced. "I know that we still have to talk this out, but I am grateful that you chose to go through with the wedding."

"You have never given up on me," she said. "I was not about to give up on you, Tyrese. We are definitely going to discuss Kennedy and all that's happened, but it won't be tonight. I will not allow her to take that away from me."

"We are going to have a paternity test," he said. "If he is my son, then we will have to put a joint-custody agreement in place."

"Whatever happens, we are in this together," Zaire stated.

"You are definitely *that* girl."

"I love you, Tyrese. That will never change." She gave him a grin. "I guess that makes you *that* guy."

Three weeks later, Tyrese walked into Zaire's office waving a gold-colored envelope. "The results are here. We'll know for sure if Matt is my child."

Zaire held her breath as she waited for him to open the envelope. She was mentally prepared for Matt to be her stepson, but she dreaded having to deal with Kennedy on a regular basis. The woman was very intrusive and had already made demands. She wanted a house in Los Angeles so that Matt could be near Tyrese, and she had requested an ungodly amount of child support.

Zaire was pretty sure that Kennedy was motivated by money, but she kept her opinion to herself.

"He's not my son," Tyrese announced.

"Are you okay?" Zaire inquired. He looked disappointed.

"I'm fine," he responded. "I just don't understand why Kennedy lied about something like this. She had to know that I would find out. I feel like I've never really known her."

"Maybe she didn't know," Zaire suggested. "It's possible that you weren't the only man she was seeing back then."

Zaire walked around her desk to stand in front of him. "I'm sorry," she whispered.

"For what?"

"I'm sorry that Matt isn't your son. I think you wanted him to be. I've seen the way you look at our nieces and nephews. You want to be a father."

"I was thinking about how confused that little boy must be by all of Kennedy's lies. He deserves the truth about his father," Tyrese said. "Yes, I want to be a father one day. But we just got married, and I want to enjoy us before we bring children into the world."

"Really?"

He nodded.

"I'm glad you feel this way because I was thinking along those same lines," Zaire confessed.

Tyrese's eyes dropped down to the envelope in his hand. "I guess we should do this face-to-face. I can't wait to hear how she explains this."

"Honey, we just have to forgive her and move on," Zaire advised. "Hopefully, Kennedy will find Matt's father and the two of them can figure out something. This has nothing else to do with us."

He kissed her. "Let's get this over with and then we can head home."

Zaire looked him in the eyes. "Why are you in such a hurry to go home?"

"I have a little five-star seduction in mind. First, I plan to—" He leaned down and whispered in her ear. "Then I'm going to..."

Zaire took the keys from Tyrese and said, "I'll drive."

His laughter echoed down the hallway.

* * * * *